FALLEN SUNRISE

Fallen Sunrise

A Shattered Sunlight Series Spinoff Novella

E.A. Chance

Darlington Publishing

eBook ISBN: 978-1-951870-22-5
Hardcover ISBN: 978-1-951870-24-9
Paperback ISBN: 978-1-951870-25-6

Cover Design by 100 COVERS

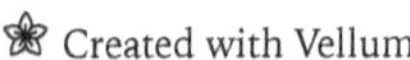 Created with Vellum

ALSO BY E.A. CHANCE

(Shattered Sunlight Series)

SOLAR FURY

HUNTING DAYBREAK

HOPE IGNITES

SHATTERED SUNLIGHT SERIES COLLECTION: BOOKS 1-3

Chapter 1

Angie Hughes set her silk blouse on the neatly folded pile of clothing before closing her new suitcase. Her husband, Grant, had insisted on buying a set of expensive new luggage for the trip to Paris to celebrate their twentieth anniversary. Angie had resisted since they'd splurged on first-class seats, but Grant said she deserved to travel in style. She smiled at how fortunate she was to have a husband who spoiled her. Most women she knew weren't so lucky.

Grant came into the room as she struggled to lift the suitcase off the bed. He gently pulled her hand off the handle, and said, "Let me get that. Your parents just got here. Go over our itinerary and instructions for the kids and dogs with them while I load the car."

Instead of leaving the room, she sank onto the bed and glanced up at him. "Are we doing the right thing leaving with that mass coronal thing on the way? From what they're saying on the news, it sounds like it could be serious. What if it turns out to be worse than scientists are predicting?"

He reached for her hands to help her to her feet. "It's a Coronal Mass Ejection or CME for short. They're like giant solar flares which cause electromagnetic pulses that can knock out power and fry electronics. They happen all the time. This one just sounds a little bigger than usual."

"What if we get stranded in Paris?"

"Where better to be stranded than the City of Light?" Putting his finger under her chin, he said, "Look at me. I know you're nervous about leaving the kids with the CME coming, but it doesn't sound like it'll do anything more than affect the internet for a few days. You know how news reporters love to sensationalize weather events. If it does disrupt the internet, that might get Allyson off her phone long enough to actually converse with your parents. What's the harm in that? In the meantime, you and I will be making out in front of our breathtaking view of the Eiffel Tower for a few glorious days. We've planned this trip for so long. We can't back out now."

Angie kissed him passionately, then with an alluring smile said, "I'm convinced. I'll be ready in ten."

She hurried downstairs, calling for her two children as she went. Her eight-year-old son, Neal, was waiting for her at the bottom of the stairs, but Allyson was nowhere to be seen. Angie was about to call for her again when her mother came up and kissed her cheek.

"Hello, dear. Get going. You'll miss your flight." Before Angie could answer, Grant bounded down the stairs carrying their bags. "Be careful, Grant. You'll fall and break your neck before you get out the door."

Grant set the bags down and gave his mother-in-law a peck on the cheek. "Just anxious to get out of here, Ruby. Where's Cal?"

"Making room in the trunk for your luggage."

"Tell Dad I'll put my carryon in the back seat," Angie called as Grant rolled the suitcases toward the door. She turned to her mom and squeezed her hands. "Are you sure you're all right with us leaving? It would take a bit of work, but I'm sure we could postpone under the circumstances."

"Canceling is out of the question," Ruby said. "You and Grant deserve this trip after all the work you've put in to get the gallery humming along. We can manage a power outage for a few days if it comes to that. Grant left enough wood stacked up out there to last the winter. Go. Enjoy yourselves and don't worry about us."

"Thanks, Mom. I just had to make sure. Want to go over the plans and instructions again?"

Ruby chuckled as she shook her head. "Not necessary, dear. I think ten times was sufficient."

Angie smiled. "Fine. You know how I am." She leaned around the corner to look into the kitchen. "Have you seen Allyson?"

Ruby nodded. "She's sprawled on the couch with earphones in, staring at her phone."

Angie sighed. "I should have known."

Allyson was a bright, cheerful, and responsible girl, but she was only sixteen. Angie knew she should only expect so much out of her, especially in a social media obsessed age. She walked up behind the couch and tapped Allyson on the head, making her jump. Allyson yanked the earbuds out of her ears and sat up to face her mother.

"Are you guys leaving?"

"We are. I wanted to say goodbye, if you can pull your eyes away from that screen for a minute."

Allyson jumped up and gave Angie a tight hug. "I'll miss you, Mom. I'm so jealous. I can't wait until I get to go to Paris."

Angie brushed a silky lock of Allyson's blond hair off her cheek. "Your day will come. I'll miss you, too, sweetheart, but we'll only be gone for ten days. We've been away for much longer before. Help Nana and Grandpa and be safe. We'll video chat tomorrow and show you the view from our room."

"Can't wait," Allyson said as she put her arm around Angie's waist to walk her to the door.

Grant and Cal had stowed the luggage and were waiting for them in the front foyer. After another round of goodbyes, Grant tugged on Angie's hand to get her moving toward the car. Neal followed them out and waved until he faded from Angie's view.

"I'm so blessed," she whispered as her father drove them to the airport. "What more could I ask for?"

ANGIE AND GRANT took the short commuter flight from the Allentown, Pennsylvania airport to Dulles International, then a shuttle to their hotel. They'd decided to spend the night in Washington, DC, since their flight to Paris didn't leave until the following evening. During their lovely day of sightseeing in the nation's capital, they did their best to avoid news of the impending CME. She'd never heard of such things as CMEs until two days earlier when the first reports started coming out. It was no small feat for them to avoid the topic in DC since it was all anyone talked about, but they refused to let it spoil their fun.

In the afternoon, they went back to the hotel to dress for the flight. Angie had gone to the hotel salon, then bought an expensive, chic new suit that was more low-cut that she usually wore, but she knew Grant would love it. Grant's extravagant mood was rubbing off on her.

They took a limo to the airport, then checked in for their flight. Angie noted there weren't nearly as many travelers as she'd expected. The security checks only took a moment and before she knew it, their plane was lifting into the sky. While they settled into their first-class seats, the flight attendant told them theirs was the last flight before the airport closed due to the CME. He said they'd made it out just in time and the plane was only two-thirds full.

Angie was grateful when Grant changed the subject and told the attendant the occasion for their trip. To celebrate, he brought each of them a glass of champagne and gave a touching toast.

During a slight delay before taking off, the captain came out to congratulate them on twenty years of marriage.

Angie felt a little like a celebrity and couldn't remember the last time she'd felt so relaxed and content. Since she and Grant had fulfilled their dream of opening an art gallery five years earlier, the demands on their time and finances had been burdensome. They were prepared for lean times, but the reality had been more stressful than they'd expected. Even so, neither of them had any regrets. For the first time, the gallery was turning a nice profit, and they had high hopes for the future.

Before Angie met him, Grant had trained under a curator at the Louvre after getting his art history degree. Angie had a museum studies degree. They'd met when Grant was hired to curate a museum exhibit in an art museum where she worked in New York City. They'd become friends from the start but initially resisted becoming romantically involved since Angie was essentially his boss. They started dating immediately after Grant was offered a curatorship at an even more prestigious museum. There they were, still soulmates and best friends twenty-two years later.

As the plane neared cruising altitude, Angie lowered her seat back and closed her eyes with a relaxed sigh, hoping to sleep during the seven-hour flight. Grant was already snoozing. Angie had always envied how easily he slept on flights. She wasn't a nervous flyer but usually had trouble sleeping. She tried running through their upcoming itinerary in her mind, but that just fueled her excitement and anticipation. She shifted gears and pictured them floating along the Seine at sunset. Logic told her it would probably be too cold for cruising the Seine in January, but it was her fantasy, so she gave herself permission to imagine whatever she pleased. Just as she started dozing off, the captain's voice came over the intercom, startling her fully awake.

"Ladies and gentlemen, I regret to inform you that we're experiencing issues with our navigational equipment. For the safety of all passengers and crew, we're returning to Dulles airport. We may experience some turbulence, so we ask that all passengers remain in their seats with seatbelts securely fastened. We'll do our best to keep you updated on the situation."

The passengers were dead silent when he stopped speaking. Angie gripped Grant's hand and stared into the blackness below. There wasn't a light to be seen, so she assumed they were either flying above cloud cover or they were over the Atlantic. They'd only been in the air for twenty minutes, but as disappointed as she was about the trip, she was more relieved that they'd soon be back on *terra firma*. Fear was starting to well up in her gut and she gripped Grant's hand even tighter. He stoically whispered comforting words to her, but she felt him tense as the plane started to shake in the turbulent atmosphere.

As the pilot began to transmit another message, there was a deafening blast and an explosion of twisting metal and fire. All the air was sucked out of Angie's lungs an instant before she was struck in the head and her world faded to black.

<hr>

Angie's brain was screaming at her to breathe. She took a gulp of air, then another. Once her breathing stabilized, her attention shifted to the searing pain in her head. The creaks and cracking of metal around her were a disorienting cacophony. She had no inkling of where she was or what had happened.

"Open your eyes, Angie," she whispered to herself. "One at a time, just open your eyes."

With intense concentration, she was able to coax her left eye open, but her right one refused to budge. She raised a fingertip to her eyelid and flinched at the touch. She took a breath and held it while she tried again. As she ran her finger over the skin, it felt like an alien face. It was so hideously swollen, she hardly recognized it as her eye socket. When she pulled her hand away, her fingertips were coated with dried blood.

She used her good eye to take in the scene around her. Through the window she saw a strange greenish glow in the sky. The only interior light was the plane's emergency lighting on the floor. She was strapped into a seat, but the passenger compartment was open to the outside, and she was beyond frozen. Gusts of frigid wind blew over her every few seconds. *What kind of ride is this? How do I get off? Where's Grant?*

She swept her gaze over her immediate surroundings in a vain attempt to make sense of what had happened. The plane had crashed landed, and the fuselage was now a twisted, broken hulk. Her seat was upright and bolted to the floor, but others were overturned, and some seats were missing all together. She recognized everyday items scattered in haphazard piles across the floor. She saw tablets, purses, shoes, papers, and water bottles.

As her vision cleared, she saw what she believed were body parts. An arm that seemed to have been separated at the shoulder was dangling from the base of one of the overturned seats. A pair of legs was lying perfectly straight in the aisle. She recognized the uniform covering them but wasn't sure why. She raised her eyes slightly to look further up the aisle and found the body they belonged to. It was the flight attendant who had toasted their anniversary.

Memories flooded back as she heard a woman screaming out a name. She put her palms to her ears to drown out the noise before she realized the calls were coming from her.

"Grant!" she screamed as her eye scanned the carnage for him.

Forcing herself to stop and wait for his answer, she closed her eyes and panted, but all she heard was silence. She clawed at her seatbelt to free herself, then struggled to raise herself to her feet, but her legs wouldn't hold her weight. She poked her thigh with a piece of splintered plastic from a tray-table and was relieved to feel the prick of pain. She wasn't paralyzed. She next ran her hands over her slacks to check for breaks or protruding bones. Not finding any, she pressed hard against the armrests and was able to stand.

Propping herself against the bulkhead near her seat, she steadied herself as she waited for the agony coursing through her head and body to subside. When the pain faded enough to allow her to concentrate, she forced herself to take another look. The scene was more horrific than any nightmare she could have imagined, but she was only focused on scanning the wreckage for any sign of Grant.

The plane was completely severed in half. In the eerie green light, Angie could just make out the jagged edge of the rear half of the fuselage resting thirty yards across a highway. A gaping hole existed where the right wing belonged in her half of the plane. The majority of seats were missing. Angie could just make out some of them scattered randomly over the field surrounding the plane. Her gut told her one of them contained Grant, but she tried to suppress these fears as she searched the nearby seats.

Doing her best to collect herself, she yelled, "Can anyone hear me?" No one answered. All she felt was cold and darkness, and the overwhelming sense that Grant was dead.

She was about to give up after finding about a dozen mangled bodies, none of which was her husband. She heard a groan coming from the section opposite the missing wing. Angie hurried toward the sound and found a man doubled over with his feet resting in a pool of blood. She kneeled beside him and tapped his shoulder.

"Sir, can you hear me? My name is Angie. I'm going to do what I can to help you."

The man turned his head to look at her and flinched at the deformed sight of her face. His skin was pale and dripping perspiration, but his eyes looked clear.

"I'm Kyle," he said between gasps. "I think my leg is broken. It hurts like hell. What happened?"

"Can you sit up?" Angie asked, afraid of what she'd find if he did.

He nodded and she helped him raise his upper body to rest against the back of his seat. She sucked in a few deep breaths before they both lowered their heads to gaze down at his thigh. A jagged edge of his femur protruded a few inches through the skin about three inches above his knee. Blood oozed from the wound, but it wasn't gushing. She didn't know that much about first aid let alone trauma care, but she took the lack of blood as a positive sign.

"Oh, my lord," he breathed before leaning his head back and covering his eyes with his hands. "I think I'm going to pass out."

She gently squeezed his arm. "You've got to stay with me, Kyle. Can you do that? I'll try to call 911, but we need to stop that bleeding while we wait for help to come. I'll find something to use as a tourniquet."

He gave a slight nod but kept his eyes closed. Angie did her best to appear calm as she frantically dug through the debris around her seat to find her phone. It only took a minute to find it buried under the inflight magazine. She almost burst into tears of relief when she turned It on, and the screen lit up. She quickly dialed 911and held her breath while she waited for the ring. Nothing happened. She tried again with the same result. Before dialing a third time, she glanced at the screen to see how many bars she had, but a red circle with a slash icon was in the spot where the signal strength indicator should have been.

Hoping it was only because her phone had been damaged in the crash, she hunted around for another cell to try. She found three but couldn't even get them to turn on.

"No luck reaching 911," she told Kyle. "My phone doesn't have a signal and the others I found are dead. Do you have your cellphone?"

He reached up and pressed his hands to his ears. "I was

listening to music from my phone on headphones when I fell asleep. No idea where they ended up."

After he described the cellphone to Angie, she got on her hands and knees to look for it. She found it where seats should have been four rows ahead. She typed in Kyle's unlock PIN, but her heart sank when the same no signal icon glared back at her.

"No signal. We must be too far from a cell tower. I'm sorry, Kyle, we're going to have to take care of you ourselves. Once you're settled, I'll go in search of help."

When he closed his eyes and gave a slight nod, she turned to find what she'd needed to treat his wound. She peeked at him to make sure he was still breathing as she searched for supplies.

While she gingerly removed the necktie from a deceased passenger, she said, "Tell me about yourself. Why were you traveling to France?"

He ignored her question, and said, "How did this happen? Did we crash? I was asleep with my headphones on. Next thing I knew, you were waking me up to this nightmare."

His words were slurred, but Angie was glad he was still conscious.

"The captain announced that we were returning to Dulles because the navigational equipment was haywire. Seconds later, a smaller plane hit us as far as I can tell, and we went down. I think we are the only survivors in this section of the plane. I haven't found my husband. I got knocked out. It's 3:10 in the morning. I must have been unconscious for a few hours."

He lifted his hands and ran his fingertips over his scalp as Angie had done. "My head doesn't seem to be injured. I must have passed out from pain."

"Look at the sky, Kyle." He slowly turned his head toward the uncovered window on his right side. "See how green it is? I think the CME hit early. That's the only explanation that makes sense."

"Excellent guess. To answer your question, I'm an aerospace engineer. I was heading to Paris to present a paper at a seminar."

After gingerly freeing the tie from the neck of a dead man lying close to her, she straightened and stared at him. "With knowledge you must have from what you do for a living, you still dared to board a cross-oceanic flight knowing the CME was coming?"

He panted from the pain for a moment before answering. "Yes. From the data my colleagues and I received, we saw no danger in it. What's happening is statistically impossible if this was caused by the CME. Guess I was wrong. The CME wasn't supposed to hit for more than a day after we landed."

Angie gathered the supplies and placed them with crutches she'd found lying next to a deceased teenage boy. "Clearly not impossible," she whispered. She leaned over him to apply the tourniquet tie, silently praying that her churning gut wouldn't get the best of her.

Never having the stomach for it, she hadn't been the one to deal with her children's scrapes and bruises. She left that to Grant. Yet there she was, forced to treat the grizzliest injury she'd ever seen. There was no choice but to get on with it before Kyle bled to death.

Kyle glanced at the tie before staring up into her eyes. "You didn't happen to find any booze, did you?"

She hurried to the galley and rummaged around for mini bottles of alcohol. She found one of vodka and one of rum. "Drink up fast to dull the pain. I don't want you to lose too much more blood."

"It may take more than this. Bottoms up." He raised the bottle in a salute to her, then gave a weak laugh which made him cringe in pain. "See if you can find two more for me and extras to use as disinfectant."

Angie hurried to the galley and rummaged through the cubbies. She found a full tray containing several mini bottles of alcohol. *I may be helping myself to some of this after I take care of Kyle,* she thought as she carried it back to him. She wasn't much of a drinker but figured taking the edge off might be the only way to keep from losing her mind.

While Kyle guzzled the booze, Angie removed his shoes, then carefully cut away his pant leg with scissors she'd found in a medical kit in the galley. Her hands trembled as she trimmed around the exposed bone. Kyle glanced at her when she leaned back on her haunches to take several long, controlled breaths to calm her nerves.

He gave her a half grin, and said, "I appreciate what you're doing for a stranger. Looks like you're not in much better shape than I am, and you could have left me here to die."

"That would have been despicable. I wouldn't have been able to live with myself."

"That just shows your excellent character. Do you have any medical or first aid training?"

She slowly shook her head to avoid aggravating her pounding injury. "None. I'm working on pure instinct and what I remember from watching *Grey's Anatomy*."

He laid a hand on her shoulder. "Just do your best. I trust you."

Angie smiled her thanks, then went back to work, hoping his trust wasn't misplaced. By the time she finished cutting away and sliding the pant leg off, Kyle was softly snoring. Angie let out the breath she'd been holding since the worst part was yet to come and it would be much easier with Kyle passed out.

She looped the tie in half and slid it under his thigh, two inches above the break. He awakened with a start as the pain coursed through his body. Their eyes met but he said nothing as she tightened the makeshift tourniquet as much as she had strength for, hoping it would be enough. He gasped for air but was otherwise quiet as he fell back to sleep.

With that most urgent task finished, she swallowed four ibuprofen tablets with half a bottle of water, then went about trying to figure out a way off the plane to go search for her husband and get help for Kyle. A four-lane highway ran between the two halves of the jet, so there was a chance she could flag down a passing car.

The door was at least fifteen feet above the ground. Much too high to jump. She spotted an emergency pamphlet sticking out of a seat pocket and grabbed it. After studying the instructions, she went to the closest door and deployed the evacuation slide. Getting down would be easy enough. Climbing back up was another story. The slide had handles at intervals along the sides.

She leaned over Kyle to tell him she was leaving, doubting he'd hear her. "I'm going for help. Don't move. I'll do whatever it takes to get us out of here."

Kyle didn't stir as she talked to him. She decided to leave him a note so he wouldn't worry if he woke up to find himself alone. She went to the overhead bin where her carryon was stored and climbed up on the arms of the seat, hoping to be able to pry it open. It took three strong tugs before she succeeded. She took a legal pad from her carryon, scribbled a quick message, then laid it on his chest where he'd be able to see it.

She downed two power bars and chugged two more bottles of water before changing into the jeans and sweater she'd packed in her carryon just in case their luggage got lost. She'd been wearing pumps with spiked heels and knew she needed something sturdier for the work she had to do. She did her best not to cringe while she pulled a pair of boots off a woman with feet roughly the same size as hers. After slipping the boots on and lacing them, she squatted beside the woman's body and thanked her. She was about the same age as Angie. There wasn't a mark on her except that her neck was turned in an unnatural angle. Angie hoped it had been a quick death.

Tears dripped down her cheeks as she said, "I'm indebted to you for this gift. These will keep my feet warm and dry. Thank you, friend."

She dried her face as she straightened and retrieved her coat.

With no more ways to stall, she walked to the slide and peered over the door's threshold. Her stomach churned at seeing how far she was above the ground. Reminding herself that Grant could be bleeding to death in the cold, and that she'd promised to bring help for Kyle, she held her breath and crossed her arms over her chest just as she remembered seeing in a safety video once. Then, squeezing her eyes shut, she jumped. Her body slid smoothly down the slide and reached the bottom in seconds. Relieved to have that behind her, she hopped to her feet and turned to face the slide.

"Not so bad," she said to no one before turning and sweeping her gaze over the crash site that covered several acres. She had no idea of where to begin her search for Grant. The smartest course of action was to start in the immediate area and work her way outward. She took out her phone and swept the flashlight beam in a circle around her, then picked what looked like the closest male passenger.

It took a full minute to work up the courage to walk the ten feet separating her from the body. As she drew near, it became obvious that the clothes were all wrong. It wasn't Grant. She bent over and blew out her breath in relief. *One down,* she thought as she moved to the next body, which was still strapped in his seat. That passenger wasn't Grant, either.

She was both grateful it wasn't him and anxious as she worked her way through the passengers scattered over the crash site. She hadn't found a single survivor. Common sense told her Grant hadn't survived the crash and hours in the freezing temperatures either, but she wasn't ready to accept that reality. After two hours of checking frozen, torn, and grisly bodies, she began to lose hope. Grant's seat could have dislodged when the planes collided and landed miles away.

She didn't want to give up, but her heart told her Grant was gone. Her chest tightened at the thought and a wrenching gasp escaped her lips. She'd done her best not to give into her emotions, but she'd reached the limit of her strength to resist. She sank to her knees on the frozen ground and sobbed out her anguish, fearing she'd never be able to stop. Within minutes, her body began to shiver so violently she was having trouble maintaining her balance.

"Get a grip before you freeze to death, Angie," she scolded herself. "It may be too late to help Grant, but Kyle is still depending on you."

Her search for Grant would have to wait. She climbed to her feet, then dusted off her pant legs and pulled her coat tighter against the freezing air before reluctantly making her way toward the road. A thick stand of trees blocked most of her view, but there wasn't a light to be seen anywhere. She wondered if the CME had knocked out the power. *At least hospitals have backup generators,* she thought as she headed to a rise in the road that would give her a better view.

When she reached the top of a small ridge, she turned in a slow circle to take in her surroundings. She was high enough to see over the treetops but there was only blackness. Either they'd crashed far away from civilization, or the CME had knocked out all the power. She had no way gauge which direction to head along the road. They could have crashed a mile or a hundred from the nearest town.

She lowered herself to sit on a fallen tree beside the road to wait for a car to pass. Her phone showed the time as 5:57 am. That meant someone might pass on their way to work. Or so she hoped. She glanced at the bars on her phone but still no signal. *Where in the hell am I?* she thought as she shoved her phone and hands into her coat pockets. She'd never felt so alone or terrified in her life.

Her eyelids drooped after fifteen minutes, and her body began to shiver from cold and the adrenaline surging through her. She got to her feet and blew on her hands while she made a circuit around her tree to stay warm. Not a single car or truck was in sight.

When an hour had passed, she saw the first snowflake flutter to the ground at her feet. Realizing she'd freeze to death if she stayed exposed to the elements, she headed back toward the plane. She needed food, sleep, and a much better plan. She and Kyle could be stuck in that plane for a day or more. She'd have to come up with a way to stay warm.

ANGIE NUMBED her mind to her pain as she climbed hand over hand back up the slide. Weak from her injuries and lack of food and rest, she fell down the slide twice as she was pulling herself up. It took her fifteen minutes to reach the top. She collapsed just inside the plane doorway and lay on her back, gulping for air.

Kyle gave a weak groan, and said, "Please, tell me that's you, Angie."

Gathering her remaining strength, she crawled to Kyle and gently laid her hand on his arm. She felt him shivering beneath her fingers. "It's me, Kyle. I'm sorry I couldn't find anyone to save us. I thought they would have sent rescue teams by now. Someone *must* be aware of the crash."

"Angie," Kyle whispered between his chattering teeth, "we need heat. It won't be long before hypothermia sets in."

Angie sat and leaned against the side of his seat and pulled her knees to her chest for warmth. "I know but how do I do that? There are two huge holes to cover, not to mention broken windows."

"Evac slides. There should be two more in our portion of the plane. Maybe you can use them to plug up the holes. Release the air in them by using the scissors in the first aid kit and haul them into the plane. They'll be heavy. You'll find rolls of tape with the emergency equipment. It's going to take time. You'd better get to work."

Angie stood and stared down at him. His face was pale, and his lips had a blue tinge. "Before I do anything else, we need to do what we can to get your body temp up. Blocking the holes won't do any good if you freeze to death first."

Angie collected all the blankets and coats she could find and dropped them in a pile in the aisle. After tucking as many as she could around Kyle, she said, "What else can I do for you?"

"I wouldn't say no to another hit of vodka. It helps blunt the pain." As she turned to grab a few bottles from the stash, he reached for her wrist to stop her. "Thank you, Angie. I mean it."

"Stop thanking me. I'm so sorry you're hurt, but I'm incredibly grateful not to be alone. Taking care of you keeps my thoughts from wandering into places I don't want them to go." He gave her a weak smile when she handed him the vodka, another bottle of water, and a breakfast bar. "Eat that and stay hydrated. I don't want you drunk so go easy on the alcohol. We need to conserve what we have. Now, let me work."

After shrugging into her coat, she easily deployed the first of the two remaining slides, then sliced the air compartments with the scissors. Once it was deflated, she hauled it into the plane. It was much heavier than it looked, or she was just weak from her injuries and lack of food and sleep. Her arms were screaming from the exertion by the time she finished, but the exercise kept her warm.

While she worked, Kyle said, "Once you're finished, we need to block the other, smaller holes and cracks to keep the cold out and figure out a way to heat the compartment. Blocking the openings will help but not enough to keep us warm until help arrives."

When Kyle paused to catch his breath, Angie said, "We can't be far from Dulles. Shouldn't help be here by now? Didn't anyone notice two planes disappearing off their radars?"

"I can't say for sure, but maybe not if it was the CME that caused the problem. Power outages might be extensive and emergency back-up sources may be damaged as well. The plane has minimal backup battery power. Think you can break into the cockpit and see if you can possibly get heaters running?"

She stopped working and shook her head as she turned to face him. "No hope of that." She shuttered as she explained the sight of a massive tree trunk jutting out of the plane's windshield. It would have been impossible for the crew to survive. "The cockpit is destroyed."

Kyle grew quiet and looked away before going on. "We'll have to come up with another way to generate heat."

"We'll worry about that after I've covered the holes and have rested some. I don't even know how long it's been since I slept."

He closed his eyes and rested his head against the seat. "I'll let you get back to it, then."

She watched him for a moment before moving to the second of the three doors containing slides in their section of the plane. The door was dented and the mechanism to release the slide was jammed. She scrounged around for makeshift tools she could use and was elated to find what looked like a crowbar. It only took five minutes to pry the compartment open. She was surprised she had the strength to do it. The slide was damaged and didn't deploy, but that didn't matter. It meant she didn't have to haul it into the plane.

After unpacking it, she measured the dimensions of the openings with a section of rope she'd cut from the edge of the slide. When that was done, she cut the slide material into sections, then taped them together. That was the easy part. Hanging them would be the challenge. Since Kyle was an engineer, she went to ask his advice, but he had fallen asleep. She hated to wake him, but their survival depended on her getting the walls installed. There was thick cloud cover and snow was coming down steadily. Three or four inches had fallen already. It must have been twenty degrees with a harsh wind blowing. Angie called Kyle's name, but he didn't even flinch.

She shook his shoulder, and said, "Kyle, I'm sorry to wake you, but I need your help."

Without opening his eyes, he said, "Don't apologize. What do you need?" She explained her dilemma in a rush. "There may be a ladder attached to the landing gear. I'm sorry to say you'll have to go out, climb the landing gear to release the ladder, then drag it back up the slide. Take a rope to make a harness. After that, feed the rope through the grommets in the slide and climb the ladder to make a pulley. You should be able to use some part of the plane to loop the rope through."

Giving her the instructions seemed to drain what was left of his energy. He dropped back to sleep before she could thank him. She hurried to the door with the inflated slide and frowned when she yanked the door open. The slide was covered with snow. She'd have to clear it as best she could on the way down so it wouldn't be too slick to climb.

Thoughts swirled in her brain as she made her way to the ground. She wondered if she had it in her to climb the landing gear, release the ladder, if there was one, then manage to haul it up the slide. With each passing hour, her regret for the hours she'd wasted in front of one kind of screen or another in her past life grew. She vowed that if she survived her ordeal, she'd devote more time to being outdoors and getting fit. She immediately realized the vow was laughable. If the CME had destroyed the power grid, there wouldn't be screens to stare at, and all other modern conveniences would be useless. Getting fit would be the least of her worries.

Though she'd done her best to fight it, her thoughts wandered to what her future would be like without Grant. She dreaded the thought of having to tell Allyson and Neal their father was dead. Grant and Neal were inseparable, and Allyson was such a daddy's girl. It would be up to Angie to make sure their family bond remained strong while they grieved their unimaginable loss. Before any of that could happen, she needed to survive her present circumstances. When help arrived, she'd ask them to take her to the nearest car rental agency so she could drive home to her children as soon as possible. There was no question of her ever setting foot on a plane again for the rest of her life.

She was grateful when her boots hit the solid ground beneath the snow. A small part of her wanted to forget Kyle and the plane and head down the highway to the nearest town. She could find the fire station and send them back to look for Grant and rescue Kyle. That would probably be quicker and safer than her trying to make their new home livable. She sighed and turned toward the landing gear supporting the nose of the plane. She'd have to postpone her journey until her current task was completed, and she couldn't consider leaving until she found Grant.

She stood beside one of the tires and gazed up with her hands on her hips. There was no ladder, but she saw a hatch door just behind the opening for the landing gear. It didn't look too hard to climb up to it. She just prayed it wasn't locked. She inched her way on top of the tire, then stretched her arms toward the hatch. It was still out of reach, so she'd have to climb higher. She made herself pretend she was a girl again, climbing trees in the yard.

Within minutes, she was close enough to touch the hatch door. She was thrilled to find it ajar. Sticking her fingers into the opening, she grabbed the edge of the hatch and pulled. It dropped open with less resistance than she'd expected, throwing her off balance. She caught herself just in time to keep from tumbling to the ground. After righting herself, she heaved her body into the dark opening and looked around in the dim light. It only took seconds to spot the ladder, right where Kyle said it would be.

She released the ladder from the bindings and lowered it through the opening. She was on the ground in moments. The ladder was much lighter than she expected. She put her arm through it and rested it horizontally on her shoulder as she carried it back to the slide. Getting it up into the plane wouldn't be a problem.

———

TWO HOURS LATER, she stood back and admired her work. She'd managed to get the makeshift walls hung with much less trouble than she'd expected. With the wind and snow blocked, the temperature in their compartment was already rising. It was far from warm, but even the small increase made a difference.

She dropped into her seat, and whispered, "It's finished."

"Wish I could get up to see your handiwork," Kyle said, making her jump.

She moved into the seat beside him and covered herself with some blankets. "I thought you were asleep," she said softly. "I've got to sleep before I pass out, Kyle. But promise you'll wake me if you need anything."

"I need one thing before you go to sleep. It's a little embarrassing, but is there something I can use to relieve myself? I'm about to burst."

Angie jumped up and took the empty ice bucket off the drink trolly. "Don't be embarrassed. If we're going to be cooped up in here in such close quarters, we're going to have to get used to this. I'm sorry for not asking sooner."

She moved away to give him privacy, wondering how long they would be stuck in the plane. At first, she'd thought it would be hours before help arrived but had to admit it could take days. She couldn't imagine surviving longer than that, especially if the freezing weather dragged on.

When Kyle said, "I'm finished," she took the bucket and dumped the contents into the toilet. Gratefully, it still flushed. She had no idea where the waste was ending up but didn't care. After checking Kyle's wound and pain level, she made sure he had everything he needed before she dozed off. He asked for a book stashed in his carryon to help distract him from his pain, then told her he had everything else he needed.

She dropped into the seat beside his with a sigh and propped her aching feet on an overturned seat in front of her. As her eyes were closing, she said, "This day has taught me how much I took for granted. I won't make that mistake after we're through this nightmare."

"Me, too. Rest now. I'll do my best to keep an eye on things."

"Thanks," she mumbled, and was asleep before she could say more.

SHE WOKE after what seemed like minutes and sensed Kyle stirring beside her. Her eyes felt like they were coated with sand, but she managed to force them open. She tapped her phone screen and was surprised to see she'd slept six hours. She turned to ask Kyle why he'd let her sleep so long but stopped when she saw the color of his face. His condition had deteriorated rapidly in the twenty hours since the crash.

She reached over and felt his forehead with the back of her hand. "You're burning up. I'll get the thermometer from the first aid kit."

Every muscle cried out as she pushed herself off the seat. She dug through the pile of emergency supplies in the steward's compartment until she found a thermometer. She scanned it across Kyle's forehead and was shocked to see it read 104.8 degrees. He was shivering uncontrollably.

"I'm freezing and on fire at the same time," he groaned.

Angie lifted his dressing and nearly retched at the condition of his wound. The skin surrounding his exposed femur was tomato red and swollen.

"Your wound's infected. You need professional medical attention and stronger medicines than what we have on the plane. I hate to leave you alone, but I've got to find someone to help so we can get you to a hospital. I may be gone for hours." She gave him as much ibuprofen and acetaminophen as was safe, then coaxed him to eat some crackers and cheese. "I'll leave everything you need within reach. I'll do whatever it takes to find help. Just promise to hang on until I get back."

"I give you my word that I'll do my best. Just hurry."

Angie bundled up as much as she could without making it impossible to move. She wasn't thrilled about journeying out alone with the sun setting but didn't have a choice. Even she could see that Kyle's condition was critical. If they were too far from a town, he might not make it.

She opened the door and was dismayed to see another six inches of snow had fallen while she slept. The only saving grace was that it had slowed to flurries. She once again cleared the snow from the slide as she went down, then followed her gut and headed west as the sun slid below the horizon. Instinct told her that was the direction they'd flown from. She'd never been the greatest at directions and couldn't rule out the possibility she was completely wrong. She guessed they were east of Dulles and Washington, DC, but in reality, they could have landed anywhere on the Eastern Seaboard.

She trudged through the snow along what she guessed was the edge of the highway. There were only two sets of tire tracts in the snow, which was disappointing. She hoped it meant people were hunkering down due to the CME and weather. She walked about two miles before the first set of headlights came heading toward her. She took a few steps away from the edge of the road so she wouldn't get hit. She was at a loss for what to do next. The person driving the car could be someone willing to help or someone who would do her harm, but at this point she didn't care. When the vehicle was a few hundred yards away, she could tell it was a large, older model truck.

Angie's heart raced as her mind frantically ran through her

options. Out of desperation, she stepped closer to the road and waved her arms, hoping the driver would stop and be willing to offer aid. In the fading light Angie could see he was a beefy man with a thick beard. He wore a heavy coat over his faded overalls and flannel shirt. His expression seemed friendly enough, though. He slowed and pulled onto the shoulder. After partly rolling down the passenger window, he leaned toward her, and said, "What are you doing out here alone in the dark? Your car dead like near everyone else's?" He had a strong Virginian accent but seemed genuinely concerned for her welfare. Angie made a snap judgment to trust him. "I survived the plane crash they must be talking about on the news. I'm on my way to find help."

His eyes widened as he stared at her. "The news? Don't you know what's happened? Power's out everywhere. World's gone black except for the fires and green sky. Everyone's saying the CME hit early. Probably why your plane crashed."

Angie had to fight back tears at hearing what the man had told her. "I was afraid of that."

He reached over and opened the passenger door. "Get in here before you freeze to death." He raised the window, and once she was settled with her seatbelt on, he said, "Name's Isaac. Where did you think you were going? There's nothing for ten miles in the direction you were headed." He pointed in the direction he was traveling. "Nearest town's two miles this way."

"Thank God you stopped then, Isaac. I'm Angie. May I have a ride to town? A man and I are the only two survivors of the crash that I've seen. He's badly injured and needs a hospital urgently."

Isaac shifted into drive and pulled onto the road. "I'll gladly take you to town but don't expect to find much. Hospital may be without power. The CME knocked out most generators. Mine's still working on my farm by a stroke of luck. I'm sorry to say you'll be on your own once I drop you off in town. I'm going on ahead to check on my parents. They live on down the way."

"I can't thank you enough, Isaac. You probably saved both our lives. You're a hero."

Isaac turned and stared out the driver window for a moment. It was too dark to tell, but Angie guessed he was blushing.

"I ain't done nothing much, ma'am. Happy to help."

They rode in silence for a few minutes before she said, "You mentioned fires. What did you mean?"

"When the CME hit, it caused sparks in all the electrical wires. Anything plugged in was fried. It happened so fast. I was in my barn when it hit and had an extinguisher handy. If not, I probably would have lost everything. My wife put out the fires in the house in time, too. There's some minor damage, but we're alive and safe. That's all that matters."

"I'm grateful you are, for all our sakes."

"Looks like some of our neighbors weren't so…"

He stopped mid-sentence and stepped on the brake when they reached the crash site. He gestured toward the wreckage before saying, "How in the world did you survive *that* with no more than a bump on the head?"

Angie held his gaze as she shrugged. She was as shocked as Isaac that she'd survived. "I can't answer that. I think I may have a mild concussion. I've got some cuts and bruises too, but other than that, yes, I'm unscathed."

Isaac whistled. "Miracle. Were you traveling alone?"

"I wasn't but I'd rather not talk about that."

He gave her a sad smile. "I'm sorry for your loss."

Aching to change the subject, she said, "Where are we? I'm from Pennsylvania and am completely unfamiliar with this area."

Isaac took the hint and pressed on the gas. "We're southwest of the airport. Shouldn't the plane have been heading east?"

"The pilot told us the navigational equipment was malfunctioning and we had to return to the airport. That's when the crash happened." Her voice softened. "That was the instant my life changed forever. Now, I just need to save Kyle, the other survivor, then find a way to get home to my kids."

Isaac nodded. "I trust you'll make it, ma'am. You're obviously a survivor."

"I appreciate you saying that. I wouldn't have believed it a day ago."

As they drew closer to the town, they began to pass empty cars stranded on the sides of the highway and debris littering the road. It reminded Angie of something Isaac said when he first spoke to her.

"You mentioned cars dying earlier. What did you mean?"

"Most newer model vehicles just stopped working when the CME struck." He patted the steering wheel. "Glad I still had this old clunker. She keeps going no matter what we throw at her."

As Isaac navigated around an overturned sedan, Angie caught a glimpse of a leg dangling out of a shattered window and turned away. She'd seen enough carnage in the past day to last ten lifetimes.

"None of it makes sense," Isaac said, drawing Angie out of her gruesome thoughts. "They said on the news that the CME would be a minor inconvenience. Nothing turned out the way they predicted. Seems like the scientists got every detail wrong. I'm afraid we're all in for a world of hurt. I just hope people from surrounding areas who weren't hit will come to our aid."

"Wouldn't you think they'd be here by now?"

Isaac didn't answer and she guessed he'd been wondering the same thing. He turned a corner and frowned when the small hospital came into view. Only the dim glow of the emergency lighting was visible. A throng of people with varying degrees of injuries hovered around the entrance.

"That doesn't look promising," Angie whispered.

Isaac stopped the truck and slowly shook his head. "No, it does not. I'm sorry to leave you like this, Angie, but I've got to see to my parents. I'll be praying for you and that man in the plane."

When Angie climbed out, he reached out to shake her hand. She took it in both of hers. Tears glistened in her eyes as she said, "You're not just a hero, Isaac. You're an angel. All my best to you and your family. I pray you find your parents safe and well."

As she turned to go, he said, "Angie, wait." She watched as he reached behind his seat and felt around. A few seconds later, he lifted a double-barreled shotgun and held it out to her. She hesitated to reach for it, so he leaned closer to her. "Take it. It's loaded. Both barrels. Can you shoot?"

She cradled it in her arms in front of her and shook her head. "I've never even held a gun."

He told Angie to cover her ears, then aimed across the empty highway and fired. After reloading, he said, "See, simple. You'll have no trouble. Just don't point at anything you don't want to shoot. I'm sorry I don't have any spare shells."

Isaac handed it back to her, then dipped his head and drove off without another word. Angie watched until the truck was out of sight, then turned to face the pathetic crowd behind her. *The nightmare is only beginning,* she thought as she headed for the hospital entrance.

Chapter 2

Angie debated for thirty seconds over whether to take the gun inside the hospital or hide it in the shrubs in the edge of the parking lot. Deciding it might get her to her objective faster, she propped it on her shoulder and headed for the teeming crowd. As she approached, most stared at her wide-eyed or scurried out of her way. She kept her gaze focused on the reception desk and did her best to block out the chaos surrounding her.

She stepped to the counter like she owned the hospital and cleared her throat. The thirtyish, dark-haired receptionist glanced up and frowned when she saw the shotgun.

She put her hands on her hips and threw back her shoulders. "You can't bring that in here, ma'am."

Angie leaned over the desk before the woman could protest again and explained her dilemma in a rush.

The harried receptionist laid her palms on the desk and glared at Angie. "You have my sympathies, Mrs. Hughes, but there's nothing I can do for you. Look around. Do you really think we can spare anyone to treat a man who probably won't survive?"

Her words were harsh, but Angie could see the hospital staff had it hands full. In running the horrifying gauntlet from the entrance to the desk, she'd passed many patients in conditions as bad as Kyle's. The receptionist went on to explain that the hospital was severely shorthanded since several staff members failed to show up for their shifts.

Angie was about to ask if they could at least spare some supplies when a woman raced up to the desk carrying a young child of about four who looked beyond hope. "Save him," she screamed. "Save my son."

Angie turned and raced out into the freezing night, then stopped twenty yards from the hospital. She sank onto a low concrete wall to gather her wits. She was at an utter loss for what to do next. Before reaching the hospital, she'd envisioned returning to the crash site in a warm ambulance with paramedics who were going to rescue Kyle and point out the nearest hotel for her. It had all been a hopeless dream. She was on her own and had remedy this desperate situation herself. She thought about her kids and parents and wondered how they were faring.

Sitting there feeling sorry for herself wouldn't solve anything, so she straightened and surveyed her surroundings. There were a few shops of various kinds that were dark and looked untouched. Next to them were a small grocery store and a pharmacy that looked like they'd already been raided. She decided to make a sweep through each of them, hoping the looters had missed some useful items.

She crossed the street diagonally and headed for the pharmacy first. She and Kyle had enough food and water to last at least a few days. Medical supplies and a solar or battery-operated heater where what they needed most. She crossed her fingers that she'd find a map of the area since she was moving blind.

She pushed through the unlocked glass doors but frowned at the sight that greeted her. It looked like a bomb had exploded in the building. Shelves were toppled and the few products that were left were scattered haphazardly around the room. She was grateful she hadn't been there during the chaos and was left wondering where to begin her search.

She wouldn't be able to find anything with the shelves tipped over in the way, so she laid the gun in a cart and lifted the closest one upright. Like the ladder from the plane, she was surprised at how light it was. She scooted it to the back wall, then went for another one. Within fifteen minutes, she had seven overturned shelves out of the way so she could begin her search.

She had no choice but to pick her way through the mess on the floor. She filled two of the three remaining shopping carts with gauze, antibiotic ointments, analgesics, and lidocaine sprays that were left. She threw a leg brace in for good measure, though she wasn't sure if she could use it with Kyle's injury. The supplies wouldn't be much help to him, but it was the best she could do.

She found no heaters or similar items. Either the pharmacy never carried them, or they'd all been looted. One treasure she was surprised to find was a local map. She tucked it in a cart with the other supplies she'd gathered.

She next braved the area behind the pharmacist's counter. There was little hope of finding narcotic pain meds, but it was possible she'd score some oral antibiotics or other useful prescriptions. Someone had already smashed the lock on the metal security screen, so she scrambled over the counter and pulled a shopping bag off a hook. Avoiding the paper bags containing already filled prescriptions, she began picking through medicine bottles and reading the labels. The names meant nothing to her. She shifted tactics and scooped anything she could find into the bags. She also took IV bags and tubing, syringes, vials, and liquids figuring they might come in handy.

With two nearly full carts, she left the store and rolled her haul to the market. She found a can opener, so she stocked up on canned meats, vegetables, and fruit. Knowing she'd need to drag the carts for two miles through snow back to the plane, she made sure not to overload them. After what she'd witnessed at the hospital, odds were slim to none that she'd run across another Isaac.

She tied one cart behind the other with twine she'd taken from the pharmacy and started for her temporary home with her treasure trove. The snow had started up again, so it wasn't easy going. She kept the carts in tire tracks where the snow wasn't as deep, knowing she'd have to hurry out of the way if a car came. None did, and she made the trip in the absolute silence of the snow-laden world.

———

ANGIE WAS DRIPPING sweat under her coat as she stood at the base of the slide two hours later. She'd been staring up at the door for five minutes, afraid to make the climb. Her greatest fear was that she'd find Kyle frozen to death. She hadn't brought help or a heater. She'd failed him. Even though she was overheated from her journey, it wouldn't take long for the cold to overtake her. She estimated the outside temperature at around twenty degrees or less. She hadn't known it got that cold in Virginia. Mustering her strength, she took hold of the rope and made the climb.

Her first impression when she stepped inside the plane was how much warmer it was then she'd expected. She'd anticipated the temperature would only be a degree or two above the outside air. *One small blessing.* It raised her hopes that Kyle was still alive. She hurried to his side and let out her breath in relief at seeing his chest rise and fall in an even rhythm. She scanned his forehead with the thermometer. It read 99.8 degrees. With the antibiotics she'd brought, he had a much greater chance of surviving until she found someone willing to help them. He'd likely lose his leg but live if he got proper medical care. Otherwise, he didn't stand a chance.

He stirred and stared up at her in confusion. "Where am I? Who are you?"

"It's me, Kyle. Angie. Do you remember?"

"It's coming back to me, unfortunately," he mumbled. "Amnesia would be a blessing at this point."

"You're fever's down. Are you feeling any better?"

He signaled *so-so* with his hand. "The pain in my leg is less, but honestly, I'm not sure that's a good thing. That probably means that the leg's dying."

Angie agreed but said, "You're alive and conscious, so there's that."

"Marginally. How long were you gone? Feels like I slept for hours."

"You did." She recounted what Isaac said about the CME, her adventure in town, and of what happened at the hospital. "We're on our own for now. I won't give up trying to find help. It's pandemonium out there and doesn't look good Kyle. I've got to be honest."

He squeezed her hand. "That's more than I deserve." When she started to shake her head, he said, "None of that. I hate to be more of a bother, but this seat is extremely uncomfortable, and my leg should be elevated. Think we could manage to stabilize the break enough to move me? You could make two of the loose first-class seats into a bed."

"I'm willing to try if you are, but first I'd like to bring the supplies I brought back out of the cold. Could you talk me through how to make a dumbwaiter system? I'm too weak to carry anything except myself up that slide."

"That will be simple enough after I've used the bathroom bucket and had something to eat."

Angie helped him take care of his physical needs, then saw to her own. She took a much needed thirty-minute rest, then got to work on her dumbwaiter. Kyle told her to use a similar system that she had for their new walls, only in reverse. She poked holes in the biggest storage bin she could find and fed lengths of rope through them. She used the hinge on the plane door as a pulley and lowered the bin to the ground. The downside of her system was that she'd have to climb down and up to load the supplies. She prayed she'd have the strength to make it.

Before stepping through the doorway, she said, "When this is finished, and you're comfy in your new bed, I'm going to build a bed for myself and settle in for a long winter's nap."

"You've earned it. No denying that. I'll stand watch while you sleep," he said with a chuckle.

"Deal," she said, laughing as she jumped off the edge and flew down the slide.

After four exhausting trips, their new stash of goods stood in neatly organized piles on the plane. Angie had dumped the medications into smaller bins and asked Kyle to go through them, hoping he was more familiar with their scientific names than she was. While he did that, she arranged two seats into a bed for him. She couldn't get them completely side by side due to the arm rests, but the second seat could be used to elevate his leg. She covered it with additional sheets and blankets to make it as warm and soft as possible.

With that finished, she made a similar bed for herself. She longed to climb into it and forget the world, but they still had the hardest and most dangerous job ahead. They had to immobilize Kyle's leg so that the bones wouldn't shift even a fraction of an inch when they moved him. He knew enough of anatomy to explain that if his femur severed the femoral artery, he could bleed out in seconds despite the tourniquet. He explained this to Angie, and as soon as the words were out of his mouth, she wished she hadn't heard them.

"No pressure at all," she joked to cover her anxiety as she prepared the materials for his splint.

"I had to make sure you understood the seriousness of what we're about to do."

"Trust me, I already knew. Tell me what to do."

"First, cut the knee brace you brought back into halves. Those will go on the outside. Smart choice to bring that, by the way. For the inside, we'll use life vests. Inflate two of them and we'll tighten them around my leg."

She nodded, then looked up at him with a smile. "I wouldn't have thought of that."

"Engineers are great at making do with what they have on hand. That doesn't mean this is going to work. Wishing I was a biomedical engineer at the moment."

"We'll make it work." While she cut the brace, she said, "We have a splint. Now all we need is a wheelchair. I don't suppose you can teach me how to build one of those."

"That's a bit beyond what we have on board. You'll have to bring a loose seat next to mine, help me into it, then drag me to the bed. It's the only way. I can't risk using the crutches. Not sure I'm even strong enough to."

"I can relate to that. I've never been so sore and exhausted in my life. Not even during that brief stint I had with a personal trainer."

"I give you permission to take tomorrow off. You won't be much good to either of us if you work yourself to death."

She pulled a life vest out from under the seat next to his and tugged on the cord to inflate it. "I'll sleep as long as I can, but we can't wait an entire day. We've got to get you to a real medical professional. This is all just a stopgap to keep things from getting worse."

"We'll just see how it goes."

Angie held up the first of the two vests. "Ready?"

Kyle cringed. "As I'll ever be."

Angie did her best to ignore her pounding heart and shaking hands as she applied Kyle's splint. The two of them worked together, deliberately and carefully adding and arranging each component.

When it was finished, Angie straightened and took several deep breaths. "That's the best I can do. Hope it's enough. How's your pain?"

He'd downed three more mini bottles of vodka before they started. He gave her a sloppy grin, and said, "Not feeling any pain at all. Am I dead yet?"

"Not yet but this isn't over. Let's finish it." Angie slid the loose seat into position next to his. "You'll have to hold my leg completely steady while we do this. Move with me. We'll take our time."

His leg was sticking out straight and resting on the armrest of the seat in front of him. Angie gingerly wrapped her hands around his calf and gave him a nod. He raised himself up with his arms and inched his body toward the other chair while Angie supported his leg. As soon as he was nestled in the other seat, he leaned forward and took hold of his leg just above Angie's hands.

"You can let go. I've got it."

Angie released his leg, then bent over with her hands on her knees. "I think I'm going to pass out."

"Breathe into a barf bag. You're hyperventilating."

She pulled a bag out of a seat back pocket and puffed into it. She felt better almost immediately. "That was the scariest thing I've ever done," she said between gasps.

Kyle shook his head. "I'm the one facing my own mortality."

"But you're drunk."

"True, but not drunk enough. You'd better get me to bed before I pass out and loose hold of my leg."

Angie gave him a quick nod, then tipped his chair back. "Hold on tight," she said as she dragged him to the makeshift bed. When they reached it, she gently lowered it flat and took hold of Kyle's leg. "Last step."

Kyle slid himself onto the bed while Angie rested his leg in an elevated position on the adjoining seat.

Kyle dropped back onto his pillow and covered his eyes with

his arm. "I can't believe that worked. I was expecting to bleed to death every second."

"Was it worth it?"

He peeked at her from under his arm. "Infinitely. This is much better, Angie. Once again, thank you."

Angie gave him a weak smile. "No more, please. We'll count that as the thank you to cover all thank yous." While she arranged whatever he might need within his reach, she said, "I'm incredibly sorry you're injured, but I'm more grateful than you know to have you here. The thought of being stranded out here alone terrifies me. What else can I do for you?"

"Climb in that bed and sleep. I insist."

She sank onto her bed and pulled the blankets under her chin. "You don't have to tell me twice."

CHAPTER 3

ANGIE SLEPT A DEEP, dreamless sleep for six hours. She woke up feeling more human than she had since the collision. She was surprised to see it was just after ten when she checked her watch. Sunshine was streaming through the windows with open shades. That meant the snow had stopped. Another good sign.

Every muscle ached, and she was far from energetic, but she felt capable of facing whatever the day had to bring. She pushed herself off the bed with a groan and went to check on Kyle. He was semi propped up, trying to focus on reading his book.

While she took his temperature, he said, "You didn't have to get up. I have whatever I need."

She ignored his comment. "Your fever is up to 101.5."

"I just took ibuprofen and a muscle relaxant. That should lower my temp."

Angie handed him the pen and tablet she'd taken from the pharmacy. "Make a note of that. We need to keep track of what you take and when." While he wrote, she glanced at his leg. The splint was gone. "Why'd you remove the brace?"

"If I remember right, it's best to keep the wound exposed with an open fracture like this. I removed the tourniquet too. The bleeding has stopped. I'm not sure if that's a good sign or bad. My pain is less, too, except for the hangover."

"I'll take that as a plus." She picked up a roll of gauze and sterile pad. "I should change your dressing."

He reached for her wrist to stop her. "No, Angie. That can wait an hour or so. Get some breakfast. Wash your face. Try to find some clean clothes."

"That does sound nice. Wish planes had showers." She lowered herself into a seat facing Kyle and tore open a granola bar package. She swallowed a third of the bar, then took a swig of water. "I have a grizzlier task to take care of before I clean myself up," she said softly. "It's time to dispose of the bodies in the plane. They're starting to smell."

Kyle gave her a sheepish grin "I wondered what that was. Thought it was me."

Angie chuckled at that. "Fortunately, no. I piled them in the corner near where the plane ripped apart and covered them with the remaining scraps of slide material while you were sleeping. But I'm still aware of them no matter how hard I try to ignore that they're there."

"I wondered about that but didn't want to say anything. You've had higher priority matters to deal with. Even as cold as it is in here, the bodies will start to decompose soon."

"I'll un-tape the base of the wall and roll them over the edge. It's not very delicate but it's efficient. I'll take the extra tarp down and cover them back up. I wish I had time to do that for all the deceased passengers."

"Someone will take care of that at some point. You can't take everything on yourself." Kyle looked down as he fiddled with a loose string on his blanket. "This is none of my business, but I was wondering if you've found your husband."

"Not yet, but I plan to make another sweep for him after I get the bodies off the plane. I'll keep looking. I need to know what happened."

"I wish I could do it in your place."

Angie felt tears pool in her eyes and quickly brushed them away. "Me, too."

She nodded, then, to change the subject, said, "Tell me about your family. Are you married? Do you have children?"

"I'm divorced. My wife left me ten years ago, looking for adventure. Apparently, being married to an engineer was too dull for her. We have two daughters. I raised them on my own after my wife took off. They're grown now and have amazing families and careers. I see them whenever they can fit me into their busy lives."

"I'm sorry to hear about your wife."

"Kind of you to say, but that's water long under the bridge. I'm seeing a wonderful woman now. She almost joined me on this trip but couldn't afford to take the time away from work. I'm incredibly grateful for that."

"Then our first priority is getting you back to her and your girls."

"What I wish most is that I had a way to get them word that I'm alive and to find out how they're doing." He paused and pointed to his leg. "That's after wishing I could get this mess fixed, of course."

Angie stood and stretched. "Goes without saying. I should get moving. There's another long day staring me in the face. After seeing to the dead, I need to find you proper medical care for you. I'm going to convince someone to come out here. Everything else can wait."

"I won't argue with that," Kyle said as he shifted to get more comfortable. "I feel the meds kicking in. I'm going to try to get some sleep while you work."

She gave a quick nod, then hurried to get at the task she'd been dreading. She gingerly tiptoed between the bodies under the bright yellow covering to reach the makeshift wall at the back of their plane section. She put on a pair of HAZMAT gloves she'd found with the emergency supplies, then ripped off the duct tape holding the makeshift covering of the gaping hole. It was a clear day at least, but still cold. Before taping the covering out of her way. She straightened and took a few deep breaths, procrastinating what came next.

She put on an N95 face mask and gloves, then went to work. She started dragging the first body toward the opening. It was much harder work that she anticipated. The bodies were rigid, slightly bloated. It was hard work moving these chunks of lifeless matter, which so recently had been a living, breathing person. Angie unceremoniously pushed the body over the side. She quickly turned away to avoid seeing the body hit the ground, but she heard the thud. Bile rose in her throat, but she gasped for a few more breaths and swallowed. She had too far to go to lose control after the first body. The job had to be done and there was no one else to do it.

She numbed her thoughts to what was happening as she took care of the rest of the twenty-five deceased passengers and their random body parts. When the grim task of removing the bodies from the plane was done, she tossed the tarp over after them before descending the slide. After arranging the bodies behind the plane and covering them with the tarp, she recited the Lord's prayer she'd learned as a child, not knowing what else to say.

Finally satisfied that she'd done her best for them, she began a second search for Grant. Nearly two days had passed since the crash. Realistically, she'd given up hope of finding him alive. With the extent of damage to the plane and the passage of time, she harbored no illusion as to what happened to him. She only hoped his death had been quick and painless. She just wanted to see him once more before giving him a respectful burial.

She searched for a fruitless hour before heading back to the plane, planning to try again before dark. She couldn't waste anymore daylight before going to find help for Kyle. After pulling herself up the slide, she re-taped the wall in place, then checked on her patient. She was pleased to see his temperature was normal.

With him sleeping peacefully, she removed her filthy clothes and cleaned off with wet wipes before putting on the outfit she'd taken from another woman's carryon. Once Kyle was rescued, she planned to search for her suitcases in the rear section of the plane across the highway.

"That's a task for another day," she whispered, then scribbled a quick note to let Kyle know she was heading out. She prayed for better luck in finding a kind soul to help than she had the night before.

It was two by the time she got on the road to town. The trek felt shorter the second time since she knew where she was going. Thoughts swirled through her head as she trudged through the melting snow. They were only hours away from hitting the two-day mark since the crash. That was almost impossible to fathom. Time had passed in a blurry rush but had also dragged on for an eternity. *How could that be?* she wondered. Not that it mattered. Time was what it was.

She felt disoriented and completely unmoored from her past life, and the only thing keeping her functioning was the driving instinct for survival. She was grateful for the necessities that kept her focused on anything other than their desperate circumstances. She needed help and had meant it when she told Kyle she would find it.

She decided to give the hospital another try, hoping things had quieted. Her heart sank when she saw that wasn't the case. It looked to her like twice as many were crowded around the ER entrance. She wove her way through the desperate throng, spurred on by the knowledge that if she didn't convince someone to listen, Kyle would die.

After what felt like breaking tackles on her way to the first-down line in a football game, she reached the reception desk.

The young, exhausted receptionist stared blankly into Angie's eyes. "What can I do for you?" she asked, clearly not wanting to hear the answer.

Angie quickly explained Kyle's condition and their situation. "My companion is in a bad way. He won't survive much longer without serious medical treatment."

The receptionist was silent as her gaze shifted to the hordes of broken people waiting to speak with her. "I didn't even know there had been a plane crash close by. It's a miracle you survived." After several moments, she trained her eyes back on Angie. "I'm not denying what you say is true, but I'm deeply sorry to tell you there's nothing we can do. Your only hope is to find a civilian to drive out and bring the man here. We can't spare a single person."

Her response didn't surprise Angie, but it crushed her hopes. "But how do I do that? I'm not even from Virginia and I don't know anyone. I don't know anyone here."

When the receptionist shrugged after staring at her for a moment, Angie turned to go. The crowd parted to let her through, glad to see one less person in line for help. After moving beyond the sick and dying, she walked past the store to figure out her next steps. Only a handful of cars had passed on her way into town. She regretted not flagging one of them down.

She walked on, ignoring her aching muscles. When she'd gone a quarter mile, she spotted a sign for the fire department a thousand feet ahead. Feeling a surge of hope, she quickened her pace. If they wouldn't help, no one would.

She'd never entered a fire station before and wasn't sure where to go. The garage bay doors were closed, so she couldn't make out if the trucks were inside. She moved past them to what looked like the main building. She hurried to the entrance and was relieved to find the door unlocked. No one was at the front desk, so she called out to let anyone inside know she was there. No one responded. She waited for a minute before calling out again. Still not getting an answer, she decided to explore on her own.

It didn't take long to find the entrance to the garage. One truck was there but the other bays were empty. Worse yet, there wasn't a soul in sight. *How could the fire station be empty during the worst catastrophe in modern times?* she wondered, as she made her way back into the main part of the building. The lights were on, and she could hear the noise from the generator churning away outside, but she didn't find a single person. Conditions in the post CME world were far worse than she'd imagined.

It was so warm and clean inside that place she was tempted to stay and forget the rest of the world. She curled up on a couch in what looked like the recreation area and covered herself with a blanket. She was out of ideas for how to help Kyle, and her body was more exhausted than what she thought it could bear. She closed her eyes with a sigh and drifted off.

The next thing she knew, someone was shaking her by the shoulder. She sat up and stared at the man who'd woken her.

He was about forty years old and tall with broad, muscular shoulders. His dark hair was close-cropped, but he had about three days growth of beard.

"What are you doing here ma'am? Are you ill or injured?" She shook her head and told him her tale. He crossed his arms over his barrel chest, and said, "I've heard and seen a thousand similar stories since the CME, except for the part about surviving a plane crash. You have no idea what it's like out there. The world is coming apart at the seams."

She stood and put her hands on her hips. "I'm aware of exactly how terrible it is out there. I'm living it. I spent the morning disposing of bodies from the crash. You can't tell me anything I haven't experienced."

"I passed the crash a few times that first night. I couldn't imagine anyone had survived, so I didn't bother to stop. There were too many people I knew who had survived the CME and were suffering. Wish I'd known you were there."

She stepped closer to him and gently laid her hand on his arm. "Make up for it by helping us now. There may still be time to save Kyle if we move fast."

He unfolded his arms and took her hand in his. "Under normal circumstances, I would do it in a heartbeat, but we're helpless here. The truck in the bay is beyond dead. The others that are out have no fuel. We've siphoned all the gas we've been able to find. We can't just empty the tanks of people who made it through the CME. Our radios aren't even working, so we can't contact surrounding stations. We're dealing with a worst-case scenario here, ma'am."

"Call me Angie," she said as she pulled her hand free and sank back onto the couch. Resting her elbows on her knees, she covered her face with her hands. "Is this real? Are these things actually happening?"

"I'm Phil." He sat beside her and put a hand on her shoulder. "I've been asking myself the same questions. It's more than my tiny brain can comprehend. I wish I had answers for you."

She lowered her hands and turned to face him. "If the fire station is out of commission, what are *you* doing here?"

He looked away and scratched his head. "My house burned down. Ironic, huh? It would be hilarious if it weren't so tragic."

Angie stared at him in shock. "Did you lose anyone in the fire?"

"No, thank the Lord. My wife and our three kids are still at her parent's house in Richmond. We spent the holidays with them. They were supposed to come home the day after the CME hit. Have no way to tell them the house is gone and to stay put."

"That's a blessing at least. I lost my husband in the crash. I haven't found his body in the wreckage yet. Our two kids are with my parents in Allentown, Pennsylvania. After I take care of Kyle, I'm going to find a way back to the rest of my family."

"My heartfelt condolences on your loss, Angie. I know that doesn't ease your suffering. In my career as a firefighter, I've seen more death than I care to remember, but never all at once like this. You hear stories about people dealing with natural disasters, but we don't really have the first idea what it's like to live through one."

"No, we don't." She jumped up and tugged on his hand to get him to join her. "Come with me to find a way to get Kyle to the hospital. You must know someone with a vehicle that's still working."

He patted the back of her hand. "I honestly don't know of anyone else who could do what you're asking. We called up all the vehicles we could round up that are still drivable. So many are in need out there, Angie. It breaks my heart to say it, but I honestly can't help you. My advice. Do what you can to get this man comfortable and go home to your children. You can't save him."

She was shocked by the words coming from this man who'd spent his life as a first responder. He'd risked his own life in saving others. If he was telling her to abandon Kyle, maybe it was time to face the fact there was no hope for him.

A battle raged in her mind and heart for a moment before she said, "I understand what you're saying, and I'm tempted to listen, but I can't give up yet. If he were my husband, I would want someone to do the same for him. It may be hopeless, but I'd never forgive myself if I left just when help was on the way."

"That's honorable, but the truth is, you'd never know."

"But I'd spend the rest of my life wondering."

When Angie started for the door, Phil reached for her hand to stop her. "Don't go. Stay with me where it's safe."

"No one is safe. Between the fires, no electricity, and lack of any medical care, we're all vulnerable." She freed her hand and continued toward the door but stopped before going through. "I'm learning that controlling what happens in life is just an illusion. The only thing truly in my power is the choices I make. I promised to care for Kyle as long as he needs me. I'm choosing to honor that commitment."

"What about your obligations to your children? Isn't there a greater commitment to care for them?"

She pushed the door open without answering his question. Her emotions were too raw and her brain too numb to get philosophical. "I've been away too long. I should get back."

"My invitation to stay will be here whenever you're ready," Phil called as she headed out of the station.

A part of her begged to curl up on that couch and pull a blanket over her head, but the better part refused to listen. She stepped into the snow and tightened her coat against the chilling wind, comforted in the knowledge that she at least had a ready refuge when the time came.

CHAPTER 4

On the third post-CME morning, Angie took her time cleaning up. It had broken her heart the previous day to tell Kyle she'd failed to bring help. To keep his hopes up, she'd reconfirmed her promise not to give up on him. But after spending a restless night with little sleep, she wondered if that had been a mistake. It was impossible to guarantee anything in the insane world they now inhabited. She regretted speaking too soon.

Kyle was growing weaker. He ate less and slept more. The skin around his wound was beginning to have a gray tinge despite the antibiotics he was taking. Even she could see he didn't have many more days of survival left.

After seeing to his needs, she said, "I'm feeling lucky. Today will be rescue day."

Without opening his eyes, he said, "I haven't known you long but enough to sense you're lying. I appreciate the effort though."

"You caught me. I'm not only lying to you but to myself too. It's the old 'fake it 'til you make it' ploy." She adjusted his pillows and blanket. "I'll try not to be gone so long this time."

"Do whatever you need to. I'll be fine. Do what you have to do."

His words trailed off as he drifted back to sleep. She had no time to waste in getting to town. As she stepped to the top of the slide, the glorious sound of a motor drifted up to her. She raised the binoculars she'd taken from a dead passenger's carryon and searched the road west of the crash site. A red beat-up jeep towing an even worse looking trailer was slowly weaving through the debris toward her. Angie held her breath, trying to decide if she should flag them down or hide. Fearing she would waste their only chance for rescue, she decided to risk it and reached for the shotgun.

After descending the slide, she hurried to the edge of the road, fifteen yards from where the driver had pulled the jeep off the road. She glared at the four brawny men inside with feigned confidence. She immediately sensed these men had bad intentions. Angie had always been good at divining people's character. Something screamed out to her that these men were not to be trusted and might even be dangerous. She saw no visible weapons, but she wasn't in the mood to take chances. The one in the front passenger seat reminded her of Isaac, the farmer she'd met on her first excursion to town, without the kindly face. When the driver reached for his door handle, Angie raised the shotgun and aimed it at his head, doubting she'd be able to actually shoot him. She would be in trouble if he called her bluff.

The driver lowered his window and stuck his head out. "Where'd you come from, lady?" Angie gestured behind her with her thumb. "The plane? You survived the crash? Are you alone out here?"

She gave a slight nod. Anticipating his answer, she said, "Did Phil send you?"

"Phil who?"

It wasn't the answer she'd hoped to hear. "Why did you stop?"

He raised his hands in submission. "Just scavenging for supplies. Things are getting pretty rough out there."

Angie moved the muzzle of the gun to the ground but kept a tight grip. "This is a graveyard. You won't find anything useful here. Phil will be here any minute with his guys to take me to town for supplies."

"Don't waste your time," one of the men called out from the backseat. "Town's picked clean."

"I'd rather find that out for myself. Move on and don't come back."

Angie's gut tightened when the driver chuckled at that. She had no idea what to do if the men got out and rushed her. She only had one shell in the gun.

"We'll go," he said after staring at her for a full thirty seconds. "But only because I can tell by the looks of you that you're worse off than we are. You better hope your Mr. Phil gets here soon." He started the jeep and drove back onto the road. He smirked as he passed. "Best of luck to you, lady. We'll probably be back."

Angie kept the gun trained on them until the jeep crested the rise. She was shaking uncontrollably by the time she lowered it, not from the cold, but from the fear.

***

ANGIE'S ANXIETY from her ordeal had subsided by the time Kyle woke and found her propped up on her bed.

"Have you been to town and back already?" he asked. "How long did I sleep?"

Angie raised her eyes to meet his. "I never made it."

"Why do I sense a story behind that comment?"

Angie recounted her frightening ordeal, then said, "It was foolish to face them. I was lucky to walk away alive."

"You weren't foolish to go with your gut, but we can't risk any more surprise visitors, Angie."

"Agreed, but how do you propose we do that?"

He watched her as he stroked his chin. "Excellent question. We build barricades across the road on either side of the crash site. It will slow people down if it doesn't stop them completely. It will at least give you a heads up before they reach our doorstep."

Angie folded her arms and stared at him. "We can build them?"

He gave a half-grin. "Right. We means you. You could even string the barricade with metal objects as an early warning system."

"How can I build a barricade alone? The downed trees are too heavy for me to move by myself."

"Use luggage and seats. Anything else scattered around the plane. Find branches light enough to drag. It could work."

Angie dreaded the idea of digging through the debris field like a ghoul but knew Kyle was right. They'd been fortunate to survive the incident relatively unscathed. They might not be as lucky the next time.

"Fine, I'll build our barricade, but we'll have to take our chances tonight. It's getting dark, and I still haven't warmed up from my last stint outside."

"Fair enough. Eat. Rest. You've earned it."

She sank onto her bed and rubbed her face. "You'll get no argument from me."

THE FOURTH MORNING dawned gray and dreary, but the winds were calm. Fearing the clouds meant more snow, she got an early start on the barricade. She began by dragging suitcases to the far western edge of the debris field. In time, she lost count of the number of trips she made. She was just glad for the distraction.

By the time she'd exhausted the supply of suitcases, she felt the first snowflake on her cheek. She turned to the mess scattered around the plane halves and increased her speed. She hadn't had time to dispose of the remaining corpses, which made the second half of the job far more distasteful. The only saving grace was that the bodies were frozen and didn't smell. She gathered the empty seats first, even going into their half of the plane and throwing the loose ones over the edge.

When the empty seats ran out, she used branches that weren't too heavy to drag to the barricade. Unfortunately, the woods were back from the road and making the round trip was wearing her out too fast. The snow was falling harder, and she was running out of daylight. She was left with no choice but to use the seats still containing bodies.

Using scissors from the emergency kit, she'd cut the seatbelts, then turn the seats over, trying not to look at the occupants. Sometimes that was unavoidable, and she knew her dreams would be filled with the frozen, dead faces of strangers that night. And for many nights to come.

By late afternoon, the snow was making it difficult to keep going. The western barricade was complete, and the eastern one was three-quarters of the way finished. Angie decided to work for thirty more minutes, then call it quits. The rest could wait for morning. *The snowstorm will offer more protection than the barricades,* she thought as she made her way to a pile of branches on the far eastern edge of the field.

As she neared the branches, she noticed three seats she'd missed. The first was empty, much to her delight. The second seat was on its side. Angie gave it a shove with her boot, then gasped in horror when it rolled upright. The body strapped to the seat was missing a head. Angie had seen plenty of missing or mangled limbs, but this was the first decapitation she'd seen. She bent over with her hands on her knees and squeezed her eyelids shut in a vain attempt to block out the grotesque image. Averting her gaze as much as possible, she tipped the chair back onto its side. That was one seat the barricade could do without.

She hesitated before heading to the third seat, which she could hardly make out through the falling snow in the dim light. One more chair would make little difference to the barricade that night, and she longed to return to the relative warmth of the plane and check on Kyle. After a brief internal argument, she decided to check it out since she was in the neighborhood.

She bowed her head to keep the snow off her face as she trotted the ten feet to the seat. As she approached, she could make out that it was on its back. Two legs covered in gray slacks and men's dress shoes were draped over the edge.

"At least you've still got your legs," she told the corpse as she drew near.

When she reached him, she brushed the snow from the seatbelt, relieved that the poor man's body still possessed a head and all four limbs. As she tugged on the seatbelt to unbuckle it, snow slid from the man's face. She couldn't help but take a peek. An animal-like moan escaped her lips the instant she recognized him. She'd found her beloved Grant.

Ignoring the gusting wind and stinging cold, she dropped to her knees beside his head and tenderly placed her gloved hands to his cheeks. His eyes were closed but his lips were curved into the faintest hint of a smile. Angie couldn't imagine what he'd found to smile about in the instant before his death, but she was comforted that he'd left the world happy.

Tears streamed down her cheeks and froze when they dripped onto his face. "How will I go on without you, love of my heart?" she whispered. "I hope you've found the warmth and love you deserve on your side. Watch after Allyson and Neal. Keep them safe until I return to them. Peace, Sweetheart. I will love you, always."

After pressing her lips to his ice-cold mouth, she struggled to her feet and dragged him out of the seat. His body was frozen in a sitting position, so she turned him on his side and covered him in a blanket of snow. She scanned the area to find something to mark the spot. She spotted a sky-blue t-shirt sleeve poking out of the snow. She yanked it out and tied it to the end of a stick, then shoved it into the snow three inches from Grant's head. The wind immediately toppled it, so she dug up three rocks to anchor it in place.

She touched her gloved fingers to her lips, then brushed them on the top of the stick. "I'll be back in the morning to give you a proper burial. Night, Babe. Stay warm."

Her reaction surprised her as she trudged back to the plane. She'd expected to have a complete breakdown when she finally found him, but she felt calm instead. Since she regained consciousness after the crash, logic had told her Grant was dead, but her heart had refused to believe it until she saw his body. Now that she had proof, a weight had lifted. It was as if she felt his presence, strengthening and comforting her. It made no sense, but she no longer felt so alone.

KYLE WAS SLEEPING when Angie made it back to the plane, and she couldn't rouse him. His temperature was slightly elevated, and his color was a sickly gray. He didn't stir while she removed his dressings to change them. She'd endured an exhausting, emotional day and didn't have the strength to hold back her tears. She couldn't deny any longer that she was losing her new friend.

After tending to his needs, she took a sponge bath and changed into a clean pair of sweatpants and a sweater she'd taken from one of the suitcases she used on the barricade. She planned to hunt for more clothes in the wreckage when she got back from town in the afternoon.

Once she was settled in her bed, she took a pad of paper and made a list of tasks for the following day. She didn't bother to add burying Grant to the list. No reminder was necessary for that task. She laid the notepad aside and closed her eyes as memories of him flooded over her.

Her thoughts wandered back to seeing Grant for the first time in the museum where they worked. She considered him handsome but not extraordinary and didn't give him another thought. It wasn't until he stayed after work one night with her to help catalog pieces that she paid him much attention. They talked for hours about their shared love of art and the city. They were inseparable after that but kept their relationship platonic until Grant left for his new job. Their first romantic night together was the highlight of Angie's life. Now, she'd never kiss him again, never hear his warm voice, or hold him in her arms. The ache of it threatened to overwhelm her.

To cope with the loss, she plucked happy events from the river of memories flowing through her mind. There was an endless supply of those, and she was deeply grateful. Her body and mind relaxed as she recalled their trip to Bermuda in the blistering heat one summer. Her last thought before drifting off was to wonder if she'd ever be so warm again.

CHAPTER 5

ANGIE WOKE to pale dawn sunlight fighting to peek through the thick clouds. It was the fifth day since the crash. Her phone battery had died three days earlier, and she'd misplaced her watch, but she guessed the time to be around seven. The snow had finally stopped, and she was in no hurry to get out of her warm sleeping bag she'd luckily found on her second trip to town. Instead, she reluctantly rolled onto her side facing Kyle, once again worried he'd died during the night. Her eyes filled with tears of relief at seeing his chest slowly rising and falling. He'd survived another day.

She forced herself out of bed to get a closer look and take his temperature. Even though he was breathing, his skin was as gray as the cloud covered sky. She scanned his forehead with the thermometer and got a reading of 96.5 degrees. His temp had gone from too high to too low in hours. Angie pulled back the blanket to check his wound and was disappointed to see he'd wet himself. That explained why his body temperature had dropped.

It was no mean feat to change him into dry clothes without moving his leg, but she managed it by moving at a snail's pace. Kyle never gave so much as an eye flutter. Angie began to wonder if he'd slipped into a coma. She covered him with clean bedding, wishing she could do more for him. His body needed fluids and nourishment, but she had no way to get them into him.

She dressed and ate in a hurry, then left Kyle to fate while she tried one more trip into town. The men from the jeep a few days earlier had said it was picked clean. She didn't doubt that but hadn't given up hope she'd find someone to help them. She was growing weaker and couldn't stay in that plane forever. Her children needed her, and she needed them.

The going was slow through the eight inches of snow that had fallen. She'd planned to bury Grant before getting on with her day, but Kyle couldn't wait, and Grant was passed needing her. She warmed as she trudged ahead trying to keep her thoughts focused on her priorities. The crush for help at the hospital had probably slowed. Patients needing help a week earlier had either recovered by then or died.

The thought made her stop in her tracks. A week had passed since the crash. It seemed like she'd lived an eternity in that plane. Kyle hadn't been conscious for two days. Was she doomed to spend the rest of her life in that place? She shook her head to clear it and took a step, then another. She had no control over her future but only what was happening in the moment. Her best course of action was just to keep moving.

She was thrilled to see the first houses come into view and picked up her pace. She made a beeline for the hospital when she reached town. Her prediction had been right. The teeming crowd at the entrance had vanished. There was a receptionist at the desk who she hadn't seen on her first two visits. She was older than the other two had been, maybe in her fifties, but she appeared rested and seemed eager to help.

Angie went up to her and recounted the weeklong saga with Kyle. "I'm pretty sure he won't last the rest of the day without medical intervention. I've done all I can for him."

She studied Angie for a moment before saying, "I'm sad to say that even if you find a way to get your friend here, we can't do much more than make him comfortable. We have no anesthesia, blood, surgical meds, or suture materials. Fuel for the generators is critically depleted. We've sent runners out to neighboring towns looking for supplies, but they haven't returned yet. I'm sorry not to have better news. Check back tomorrow. Maybe the runners will be back with what we need to treat your friend."

Angie's heart sank. She doubted conditions were any better in surrounding towns. Bigger cities probably had better stockpiles but wouldn't be willing to part with them.

"I appreciate your honesty," she said. "If Mr. Bradley survives until tomorrow, I'll come back."

"Have you tried the fire station? They might be able to bring you both into town. That would at least give you a warm place to sleep, and we could monitor Mr. Bradley's condition for you."

Angie nodded. "I went there several days ago. They weren't able to help." *Or willing,* she thought, remembering her encounter with Phil.

"I'd advise you to try again. Our supplies may be depleted, but we've become more systematic and organized in dealing with the situation than we were even a few days ago."

"I'll do that," Angie said as she turned to go.

"Wait," Paige whispered. Angie stopped and faced her. "There might be one thing I can do to help. Stay here. I'll be right back."

Angie raised her eyebrows as she watched Paige scurry off. She doubted the woman had anything to offer that would make the least bit of difference to Kyle. She slumped into a chair and closed her eyes. It had never occurred to her for one instant in her life that she'd live to witness the end of the world. "Lucky me," she whispered. Grant and the possibly thousands of others who had died were the ones she envied. They weren't left behind to endure the hell she was living through.

She heard Paige coming back, so she opened her eyes and sat forward. A man wearing a white doctor's coat was following her.

He walked up to her chair and extended his hand. When Angie shook it, he said, "I'm Dr. Hamilton. Paige told me about your situation." He held a small paper bag with the pharmacy logo printed on it. "I would never do this under normal circumstances, but here is one of our last vials of morphine. Use this to ease your friend's pain. Instructions are on the vial. Have you ever given anyone a shot?" Angie's eyes widened as she shook her head. "It's easy. I know you can do it." He handed her the bag and turned to Paige. "Ask Janice to find a home injection instruction sheet."

Angie's hand shook as she reached for the bag. "What if I give him too much? What if he's allergic?"

"By the sounds of his symptoms, I don't think there's much you can do to hurt him now. We're out of syringes, unfortunately, but you might find some in the plane's emergency supplies. Don't bother with the pharmacy. We've taken all they had."

Paige came back and handed her a folded piece of paper. "Everything you need to know is written there."

Angie got to her feet, hugging the bag and instructions to her chest. "I'm very grateful. It's been torture seeing Kyle suffering so much pain. He's been brave but it's taken a toll. I'll make sure to tell him of your kindness."

"Wish I could do more," Dr. Hamilton said as she headed for the door.

Once outside, she turned to give the fire station another try. The garage doors were still closed and the truck bays empty. She went to the main building but found no one. The only lighting was the emergency exit signs and the building was silent. She called out for Phil but got no answer. The couch called out to her, but she ignored it and rummaged in closets and cupboards for first aid kits or other emergency supplies. She found nothing. Not even a single syringe. The fire station was in as dire a situation as the hospital.

She was tempted to wait for someone, anyone, to return but

knew that could take hours. She had to find syringes to administer the morphine, then get back to Kyle. She once more turned her back to the warmth and peace of the station to head out into the cold. Her disappointment at failing Kyle a third time lessened a bit at seeing the clear bright sky.

She made stops at the market and pharmacy in the hope that looters had missed a pack of syringes. In the end, it had only been more wasted time. Her last hope was that she'd find at least one syringe on the plane. She hadn't looked for any before since she'd had no use for them. It was possible a passenger carried a syringe for insulin or some other medication. That hope drove her to increase her pace as she trudged back to the plane.

KYLE WAS HANGING on when she made it back, but she still couldn't rouse him. As she searched the plane for syringes, she wished she'd asked Dr. Hamilton for IV fluid bags and asked Sandy to show her how to use them. Kyle hadn't had any food or water for more than two days. After an unsuccessful hour searching, she admitted defeat. She convinced herself that the morphine probably wouldn't have made much difference to Kyle. He seemed oblivious to the world around him, so she doubted he was feeling any pain.

Not willing to sit idly by and watch Kyle fade away, Angie grabbed the trusty folding shovel she'd found on the plane and descended the slide. After clearing a three-foot circle in the snow, she lined the perimeter with small rocks she'd found around the crash site. She next gathered twigs and branches, then piled them inside the circle. When that was done, she doused her creation with lighter fluid and tossed a lit match on it. A glorious fire roared to life.

While the bonfire burned, she dragged the biggest branches she could find and used the ax from the plane to chop them into logs small enough for the fire pit. After stacking them out of reach of the flames, she dropped into a seat she'd removed from the barricade and admired her handiwork.

She'd refrained from starting fires up to that point to keep from alerting anyone passing by, but it no longer mattered to her if anyone noticed. As far as she cared, anyone who wanted to steal all their goods and murder her was more than welcome. She'd even torn up a white sheet and written SOS on it in large black letters with a marker to wave at passersby. Not that she'd seen any of those for two days. She tied the flag to a stick and rested it against the arm of her chair. All that was left to do was enjoy the brightness and warmth of her fire and wait for whatever might come.

Fifteen minutes later, she was roasting marshmallows on a pronged stick and admiring the spectacular Northern Lights show when she spotted a pair of headlights off to the east. "Here they come! Everybody get ready!" she shouted, then laughed at her joke. "Get a grip, Angie," she told herself as she pushed out of the chair and grabbed her flag.

She raised her binoculars to her eyes and focused them on the headlights. An old truck was weaving through the debris at a breakneck clip. *They're in a hurry to rob me*, she thought as she lowered the binocs and began waving the flag over her head. The truck screeched to a halt when it reached the barricade. Angie held her breath while she waited for the occupants to get out and come for her.

When nothing happened for more than a minute, Angie let out her breath. She dropped the flag and put the binoculars back to her eyes. A small woman with red, curly hair in the driver seat was arguing with a fair-haired man in the front passenger seat. The man gave a shrug and opened his door, signaling that the argument was over. The woman climbed out and got into stride beside him. He kept trying to get ahead of her, but she wouldn't let him. It was like watching *Mario Kart*. Angie would have found it comical if she weren't so terrified.

She didn't see any weapons but that didn't mean they weren't armed. She raised her hands in surrender and made her way toward them through the debris. "You're the first people in a week willing to stop," she said, lying to them when they reached her. "Thank you. My name is Angeline Hughes. Angie. There's a man on the plane whose leg is severely injured. I've managed to keep him alive, but he's not going to make it much longer."

The man stepped between her and the woman. "You've been living in that plane for a week?"

"Yes. It's been a hellish nightmare, believe me. Can you help us?"

"Who were the other people passing by?" he asked cautiously. "How many were there?"

"Mostly families or truckers, but there was this one group of thugs who were about to stop until I pointed my shotgun at them."

He took a step closer. "Where's the shotgun?"

The woman nudged him out of the way with her elbow, and smiled as she said, "We'll do what we can. We're doctors, but most of our medical supplies were stolen from us earlier today. Do you have any on the plane?"

Angie's legs gave out and she sank onto a stack of suitcases. "You're doctors?"

The man poked his head around the woman, and said, "Surgeons."

"It's a miracle," Angie whispered. "I took what I could from a pharmacy about two miles from here. I don't know if it's what you need."

"We'll find out," the woman said. "Help us get what little we have from the truck."

Angie stood and wiped her eyes. "You're angels sent straight from heaven."

As they walked to the truck, the woman said, "I'm Dr. Riley Poole. This is Dr. Cooper, but he'll insist you call him Coop. Call me Riley."

Angie shook her hand. "Overjoyed to meet you both. Sounds like you've been through quite the ordeal yourselves."

She could feel Riley's eyes on her. "I won't deny it's been an adventure, but nothing like surviving a plane crash."

When they reached the farm truck that had seen better days, Coop tapped his knuckle on the passenger window. Angie flinched when two teenage girls popped their heads up and stared at her with wide eyes.

When the older looking one rolled down the window, Coop said, "Hannah and Julia, stay here until we come for you. Keep the doors locked and stay down under the blanket. You know the drill."

The one called Julia nodded and covered herself and Hannah with a blanket. "Sure, Coop."

Riley patted her head. "Thanks, sweetie. This shouldn't take long."

Angie felt the tension drain from her. She'd made a choice to go along with the doctors, but after seeing the girls, she was certain it was safe to trust them.

Riley and Coop filled backpacks with the supplies they'd need. Angie hoped they could work some magic to save Kyle, but her gut told her it was too late.

"Do you mind telling us what happened?" Riley asked as they made their way back to the crash site.

"My husband and I were flying from Dulles to Paris for our anniversary when the CME hit. A smaller plane struck us, and both crashed. My husband didn't make it."

The last words caught in her throat, and she paused. Riley put an arm around her waist. "I understand. My husband died in a helicopter crash three years ago."

Angie nodded and gave her a knowing look. "I have a teenage

daughter and an eight-year-old son. I left them with my parents in Allentown, where we live. I haven't stopped thinking about them for a second since the crash. I've just been fighting to stay alive. I've got to get back to them no matter what it takes."

Riley stared at the ground as they walked. "I left a son and daughter with my parents in Colorado Springs. It's torture being separated and not knowing what's happened to them."

Coop rubbed Riley's shoulder as he turned to Angie. "What about the injured man? What's his name?"

"Kyle Bradley. He was flying to Paris on business. Kyle and I were the only survivors from either plane as far as I know."

Coop rubbed his chin as he studied the plane. "It's incredible anyone survived that."

When they reached the slide, Angie grabbed hold of the rope and pulled herself up, hand over hand, to show the others what to do. Coop followed her. Riley went last. Angie was impressed at how well the doctors climbed the slide on their first try. They were clearly in better shape than she'd been a week earlier.

Once inside, she led them to Kyle. He was still unconscious but moaned as they approached. The doctors leaned over and silently studied him for a moment.

Riley finally straightened and gave her a sympathetic smile. "Would you mind waiting in the truck with the girls while we treat Kyle? I don't like leaving them out there alone."

"I'd much rather be there than here. The medical supplies from the pharmacy are in that backpack on the floor next to Kyle," she said, then practically dove down the slide and rushed to the truck as fast as her legs would carry her.

The girls had seen her coming and had already opened the back door to let her in when she reached the truck.

"There's room back here with us," Hannah said, as she scooted to the middle and patted the seat next to her.

Angie watched her for a moment before answering. The girl looked to be about eleven or twelve. She had a darling face but was too thin. Her large dark eyes were slightly sunken their sockets, and Angie read a touch of melancholy there. Her pale skin was nearly translucent, but she had beautiful black hair woven into braids. She reminded Angie of what she'd imagined Snow White would look like. She didn't resemble Coop or Riley in the least.

Angie felt Julia watching her, waiting for an answer. Julia had silky, light brown hair and intense, hazel eyes. It was clear she never missed anything. She had a hint of Riley's mouth and nose. The most striking thing about her was the ugly, swollen bruise on her left cheek and eye. There was a story there that Angie wasn't sure she wanted to hear.

She gave Hannah a half grin. "That's kind of you, but would you mind if I sit in the front closer to the heater until your parents get back?"

"They're not my parents," Hannah said without emotion.

Julia put her arm around Hannah's shoulders, and said, "You can sit in the front. I bet you're freezing. We know what that's like."

As Hannah pulled her door closed, Angie hurried around to the front passenger seat. Once she was settled, she held her hands out to the heater vent. Nothing had ever felt so glorious.

She sank back against the seat and closed her eyes, but flinched when Hannah said, "What's your name?"

Angie reluctantly sat forward and turned to face her. "Angie Hughes. I'm sorry for not introducing myself."

Julia nodded. "It's okay. We get it." Putting her fingertips to her bruised eye, she said, "It's hard to remember to be polite in this new insane world. We've been through some stuff. What are you doing out here all by yourself?"

Angie told the girls about the plane crash and Kyle, taking care to leave out the worst parts. "I think we both would have died if the four of you hadn't come along."

Hannah looked down and fiddled with a string on her coat

sleeve. "I hope they can help your friend. Too many people have died already."

"We don't know what happened to Hannah's parents," Julia said softly. "Riley's my mom. Coop's a new friend we met right before the CME." She paused, lost in thought for a moment. "It's weird to think about. Feels like we've known him forever."

Angie nodded. "I know what you mean. I feel the same way about Mr. Bradley. Do you live near here? Where are you coming from?"

Julia leaned forward and rested her arms on the back of the front seat. "None of us are from here. We live in Colorado. I was in DC at a medical conference with my mom. Coop was in charge of it. That's how we met him. He and Mom are totally into each other," she said. She and Hannah both giggled at that. "I'm glad for Mom. She'd been so lonely since Dad died."

Angie gave them a weak smile. "And what about you, Hannah?"

"I'm from California. I was at the same hotel. My mom and dad left me there while they went house hunting. The CME hit and they never came back. Julia and Riley made me part of their family."

Angie fought back tears at hearing the girl's gut-wrenching tale. It made her wonder what her kids must be suffering, not knowing what happened to her, or if she was still alive.

She wiped her cheek with the back of her hands, and said, "I'm sorry about your parents, Hannah, but I'm glad you found such good people to care for you."

The girls peppered her with questions while they waited for Riley and Coop. All she wanted to do was close her eyes and rest, but she didn't want to be rude to these people who had rescued her.

When thirty minutes passed, and she was getting anxious about Kyle, she looked up to see Riley and Coop lowering him down the slide in a blanket they'd tied with ropes. His face wasn't covered, so Angie took that as a good sign. She jumped out of the truck and went to help carry him.

As soon as they had him laid in the covered truck bed, Coop said, "We'll take care of him from here. If you'd like to come with us, we'll wait while you get your belongings from the plane."

"I'd love to go with you. There's nothing for me here." She turned to go, then stopped and laid her hand on his arm. "How is Kyle? Does he have any chance of surviving?"

He gave her a guarded look, which was answer enough, but he said, "It's hard to predict accurately without proper medical equipment, but I wouldn't get my hopes up. His condition is grave. We've given him morphine. He's not suffering any pain."

Angie knew he was sugarcoating Kyle's condition for her, but she appreciated it. Her gut had been telling her for the past twenty-four hours that he wasn't going to make it. Her one comfort was that she'd honestly done all she could for him. She thanked Coop before going to get her few meager belongings.

She only took what she could carry down the slide. There would be time to replace her clothes and luggage later. All she wanted at that moment was to get closer to her children and as far away from that plane as she could. The time would come when she'd be ready to return and bring Grant home, but she had a long road to travel before that day came.

She hurried back to the truck with her pack and climbed into the front seat with Coop. Riley rode in the back to monitor Kyle.

Coop had cleared a path in the barricade. As he carefully maneuvered the truck through the opening, Angie said, "Where are we going?"

"We're trying to find a place to sleep for the night, if that's possible. We'll stop as soon as I feel it's safe."

She nodded as she watched the plane fade in the truck's side mirror. "I don't have words to express how grateful I am that you crossed my path. I'll always look on you and Riley as my saviors."

Coop gave her a half grin, then ran his hand through his hair. Angie could see she'd embarrassed him.

"That might be going a bit far, Angie, but we're grateful we could help. We've only been on the road for a day, and it's been the most harrowing of our lives. Let's all pray the worst is behind us."

"Amen," she whispered, then closed her eyes and drifted off to the first warm and safe sleep she'd had in a week.

Chapter 6

ANGIE WOKE to the sound of wheels crunching on gravel. She sat forward and rubbed her eyes to get a look at where they'd stopped. Coop had parked in the driveway of a quaint yellow cottage surrounded by forest. There was no light coming from inside and no smoke from the chimney. She crossed her fingers for luck that the house was empty. All she wanted was to get a fire going and sleep warm and safe for the rest of the night.

"How long have we been driving?" she asked Coop as he unbuckled his seatbelt.

He rubbed his face and shook his head before answering. "Just over two hours. I can't keep my eyes open another minute. If we can't stay here, you or Riley will have to drive. We won't get far. The tank is almost on empty."

As Angie climbed out and the girls followed, it occurred to her that she hadn't thought about gas. With the power out everywhere, there was no way to pump it out. People would have to figure out a way to siphon it out of the underground tanks.

The four of them walked to the back of the truck. The girls danced around to stay warm while Coop opened the tailgate to let

Riley out. Angie stepped away from the others and turned her back to them, dreading what Riley might have to tell her.

Riley quietly approached her, and said, "Kyle didn't make it. There was nothing we could do. I'm truly sorry."

Light from the aurora glinted off the tears pooling in Angie's eyes. She wiped them with her sleeves, and said, "This is silly. I knew him for less than a week."

Riley put her hand on Angie's shoulder. "A few days can feel like a lifetime in a crisis. You were kind to stay and try to save Kyle. No one would have blamed you for leaving him to die."

Angie spun around to face Riley. "I never could have done that."

Hannah took her hand as she and Riley rejoined the group. "I'm sorry your friend died, Mrs. Hughes. You can be part of our family now. Coop and Riley will take care of you."

Angie was touched by the kind comment but couldn't miss the glance that passed between Coop and Riley. She could already tell they were the kind of people that would never abandon her on the side of the road, but that didn't mean they planned to take her along with them. They likely planned to deposit her in the first safe place they found.

Coop closed the tailgate and shoved his hands in his pockets. "We'll take care of Kyle's body in the morning," he said, letting Hannah's comment drop. "Let's see if the occupants of the house are willing to put us up for the night."

"The house is cute," Julia said. "Like a cottage from a fairytale."

"Let's hope there's not a wicked witch inside," Coop mumbled. "Riley and I will check first. The rest of you wait in the truck."

"Back in the truck," Julia grumbled as she opened the door. "I'm sick of the truck."

"Be grateful we have it," Riley said, as she followed Coop to the front door.

"Come on girls," Angie said as she got into the back seat. "It's probably freezing in the house. At least we have heat in the truck."

Julia frowned but climbed in behind Hannah. "That's better than nothing."

To distract them while they waited for Coop and Riley, Angie said, "Coop told me you've had a rough time of it since the CME. Do you mind telling me about it?"

"Is it okay if we don't tell you tonight?" Hannah asked. "It's a long story and I don't want to think about it."

Angie nodded. "Of course, you don't have to tell me. How about if I tell you about my family?"

"Sure," Julia said. "Were you flying alone when the plane crashed?"

Angie's breath caught in her throat. Her emotions were as raw as Hannah's and Julia's, but she was ready to talk about Grant. She told them of Allyson and Neal, and the anniversary trip. When she told them about finding Grant in the snow, Hannah covered her face and silently cried into her hands.

"Your husband died in a plane crash like my dad," Julia said quietly. "It was three years ago, but I still miss him." She paused and reached for her door handle. "They're taking forever. I'm going to go see what's going on."

"You should wait here like Coop said to," Angie called after her. Julia ignored her and threw the front door open, then slammed it behind her.

Hannah blew her nose into a paper towel, then said, "Julia's always doing stuff like that. You better get used to it."

Angie chuckled at that. "I'll do my best. She reminds me a little of my daughter."

Julia burst back out through the doorway and ran toward the truck a minute later. Yanking the truck door open, she said, "We get to stay! Mom and Coop want us to unload the truck. They said they have to take care of something inside, then they'll help us."

Angie was overjoyed at the news that they were staying. She unfolded her aching body out of the truck once more and directed the girls to help her unload the gear. By the time they emptied the contents of the bed into a pile on the frozen ground, Riley came out and signaled for her to join her on the porch.

When Angie reached her, she said, "The owners of the house were an older couple who passed away inside. One was diabetic. The other was on an oxygen concentrator. We're going to hold a brief memorial for them later, but you and the girls can start bringing our belongings inside. We'll join you once we're finished tending to their bodies."

Angie nodded and returned to the truck. *More dead bodies*, she thought as she joined the girls and explained what was happening. Death was a new and unwelcome reality in their everyday lives. They had no choice but to get accustomed to it. She hoped her children were more shielded from it than these innocent girls.

"Horrific," she said without thinking. Julia and Hannah turned and stared at her with raised eyebrows. "Sorry. I was just thinking of those poor people in the house."

Julia shrugged, then picked up another load to carry inside. "We've seen tons of dead people."

She said it so nonchalantly that Angie had to fight tearing up.

"That's something else you better get used to," Hannah said as she passed on her way into the house.

Angie leaned against the tailgate and stared out into the darkness. As hellish as life had been since the crash, life outside her bubble seemed worse. She envied Grant for the second time. If not for her maternal instinct driving her to get to her children, it would have been easy to just walk off into those woods and let the end come.

She shook her head to clear those dark thoughts. She had

found these good people and she did have her children waiting. She straightened and dusted off her pants. It was time to take a cue from Julia and Hannah and just get on with life. In the end, there was no better choice.

AFTER GETTING a roaring fire going and saying a few touching words for the deceased owners of the house, Coop and Riley heated a meal of canned stew and toast over the fire. It was the first hot meal Angie had eaten since the day she and Grant left for Paris. She savored every warm, delicious bite. When their feast was finished, they each climbed onto the mattresses they'd dragged into a den with a fireplace at the back of the house. With a full belly and warm body, Angie drifted off minutes after wishing the others goodnight.

After what felt like moments, she heard a girl scream, "Fire! Everybody up!" She thought she'd dreamed it until she heard it the second time. She bolted upright on her mattress, then scrambled to her feet at the sight of five-foot flames dancing across the room. The fire blocked the door within seconds. As Angie desperately tried to figure out what to do in her sleep-addled brain, she caught sight of Coop opening a window.

He motioned to her, then yelled, "This way," over the roar of the flames.

She bounded across the room in four steps and dove through the open window after Hannah, landing hard on the snow-covered lawn. After Riley jumped out, Cooped lifted Julia through the opening. Flames blazed on the leg of her sweatpants. Riley rolled Julia in the snow to douse the fire. Coop dove out just in time as the flames licked the windowsill. He rolled to a stop, then jumped to his feet to check on Julia. Satisfied that she wasn't harmed, he sank into the snow next to Angie.

The five of them stared at each other in shock as they tried to catch their breath. The fire flared up to the roof, causing a beam to go crashing to the floor. They came to their collective senses, scrambled to their bare feet, and ran toward the road to put space between themselves and the blazing inferno. They stood on the frozen ground and watched in horror as the fire engulfed their sanctuary and the rest of their earthly belongings.

Angie glanced at Hannah, who was shivering uncontrollably. "We can't stand out here freezing to death. We need the truck, Coop. Please don't tell me the keys are in the house."

"No, I left them in the truck," he shouted as he raced toward the house.

He had the truck up to the road in a flash. Everyone gladly climbed in except for Julia. Inexplicably, she turned and headed back toward the fire.

"Julia!" Riley screamed, but her daughter ignored her.

Coop flew out of the truck and ran after her. Angie watched in stunned silence at the scene taking place twenty feet away. Coop reached for Julia's arm, but she pulled away and started for the house. Coop caught her and shook her by the shoulders.

"She's in shock," Riley whispered.

Hannah put a hand on her shoulder. "Don't worry, Riley. Coop will get her."

The front wall of the house caved in and sent sparks flying toward them. Julia jumped out of the way and took Coop's hand to let him lead her to the truck. He opened the door and helped her up to the seat beside Hannah.

Riley opened her mouth to speak, but Coop raised his hand to stop her. "Don't ask," was all he said.

Angie couldn't fathom what was happening, so she turned her attention to their temporary sanctuary. As she did, there was a deafening crash as the roof disintegrated and crashed to the ground. She glanced at Julia to see her reaction, but she just rested her head on the cold window and closed her eyes.

Coop slowly moved the truck closer to the house but kept far enough away to avoid sparks. "The fire and our collective body heat will keep us warm until morning, so we won't waste gas running the heater. Once the fire's out, we'll see if there's anything to salvage. We'll move on and look for a new place to restock. In the meantime, I suggest we get some sleep."

Angie doubted she or any of the rest of them would be able to close their eyes after the terrifying ordeal they'd just lived through. She was wrong. As she stared into the flames, her eyelids began to droop. Her exhaustion won over her anxiety, and she was asleep within minutes.

———

ANGIE FELT sunlight on her face before opening her eyes. She took a moment to enjoy the sensation before fully waking up. She'd slept with her head against the window and had a kink in her neck. She looked around the cab as she massaged it. Coop and Riley were gone, but Hannah and Julia were out cold. She opened the door as quietly as she could and went to find the others.

Embers stilled glowed where the house had been, but the temperature had plummeted. She tiptoed to the back of the truck in her sock-covered feet and found Riley reaching for something in the bed.

"I tried not to wake you," she said.

Angie shook her head. "You didn't." She looked at Riley's sweater-clad feet and raised her eyebrows. "Glad I sleep in socks, though they won't keep my feet warm for long. My bladder's about to burst. You don't happen to have a port-a-john, do you?"

Riley held the bucket up by the handle. "Best we've got." She set the bucket down and leaned against the truck, staring at the smoking remains of the house. "Still glad we rescued you?"

Angie gave a half-grin and leaned against the truck next to Riley. "Believe me when I say yes."

"I can't imagine what a nightmare it must have been living in that plane for a week."

Angie closed her eyes. "No, you can't." Riley tenderly rested her hand on Angie's shoulder. "But that's over, and I'd like to use that bucket now if you don't mind."

Riley pulled a dirty, half-used roll of paper towels from the truck and handed it to her. "All yours."

Angie crossed the road with the bucket and went a short distance into the woods for privacy. It made her appreciate the plane's toilet. After using the bucket, she lowered herself onto a stump for a moment to reflect alone before rejoining the others. Everything happened in a blinding blur in the past twelve hours. Just when she'd resigned herself to spending the rest of her life in that blasted plane, Riley, Coop, and the girls showed up to rescue her. Kyle had died. Worst of all, she'd lost her husband. She was a widow. They'd found the perfect sanctuary and had discussed staying for a few days to catch their breath. Before they could, it burned to the ground, leaving them in search of shelter.

She was beginning to wonder what she'd done to anger the Fates. She was cold and hungry and didn't own a thing in the world but the clothes she wore. She'd experienced fourfold the turmoil in the past eight days than she had in her entire life. She tried to be optimistic in front of her new friends, but it was an act. She told herself there would be another shelter. This time she would keep a better eye on the fireplace.

She got to her feet with a grunt and headed back to the truck. Her spirits lifted as she picked her way through the sunlit woods. As dire as their situation was, she wasn't alone, and that meant more to her than anything.

After they each took a turn with the bucket, Coop emptied the contents onto the glowing embers of the cottage and rejoined them after closing the tailgate.

"Our top priorities in this order are shoes, warm clothing, water, and food. Do you all agree?" The four women nodded. "I got out of the fire with my gun and a full cartridge, but we lost the ammo, so we need to stay close and be alert. And let's avoid any more accidents."

He winked at Julia, which baffled Angie, but she didn't ask what it meant. Coop put the truck into gear, and they were off to their next adventure. They wove through nearby neighborhoods looking for one empty house that would suit their needs. They passed several burnt-out shells of houses. Angie shivered at seeing each one. They passed others that were clearly occupied or had been ransacked.

As Coop slowly drove down one street, Angie spotted a brick farmhouse missing a front door. "That one looks promising," she said.

"Didn't you notice there's no door, Angie?" Coop asked.

"I'm not talking about the house. I meant that big workshop near the woods in the back," she replied.

Coop moved the truck so they could all see the large metal building that backed up to the tree line. It looked like a woodworking shop. A heavy padlock hung from the door handle.

"That's definitely worth a look," Coop said. "Riley, please grab the crowbar and come with me."

Angie waited in the truck with the girls and was relieved to see Riley waving for them to come join her five minutes later. Hannah and Julia were out of the truck in a shot, but Angie followed at a slower pace. When she made it to the workshop, her hopes soared. They'd discovered a treasure trove. Riley pointed out three cases of bottled water, two full gas cans, and a trunk full of old hunting clothes. Best of all there were enough boots for all of them. They weren't the right sizes, but they beat the hell out of bare feet.

They rummaged through the workshop for another hour and came away with a shotgun, three boxes of shells, ropes, an ax, and a tarp. The one thing they didn't find was food, but they had enough gas to drive to the nearby town and scavenge. They carried their loot to the truck and loaded it while Coop poured the gas into the truck's tank. They were all much more optimistic as they got under way.

While they drove to the town called Warrenton, Riley explained that they were headed to her uncle's horse ranch in southern Virginia. Angie was disheartened to hear that since she needed to travel north. When she grew quiet, Riley asked what was wrong.

"I won't be going on with you after Warrenton," Angie said.

Riley turned and peered at her over the seat. "You're staying?"

"Yes, if I can find someone willing to take me in."

"You can't leave us," Hannah said and took Angie's hand in hers. "You're part of our family."

"Leave her be, Hannah," Riley said, without taking her eyes off Angie. "Mind if I ask why?"

Angie lowered her head and covered her eyes with her hand. "I have to find a way to get home to my children. They don't know about their father or that I'm alive."

Riley studied her for a moment, then said, "I understand that you're eager to get back to them, but is it worth taking up with strangers who could be dangerous?"

Angie looked her in the eye. "You were strangers. There must be others like you. I'm banking on the hope that not everyone has turned evil."

"Don't count on that," Julia said. "You're the only nice person we've met. Come with us to my uncle's ranch until it gets warmer. Then, we'll help you get home."

"That's kind of you, Julia, and I appreciate all you've done to help. I couldn't have survived another night in that hellish plane any more than Kyle could, but you're heading too far in the wrong direction. Look how long it's taken you to get this far from DC, and you've been on the road for two days."

"Can't argue with that," Coop said. "We'll help you find a safe group to travel with, if such a thing still exists."

"I'll miss you," Hannah said and rested her head on Angie's shoulder.

They rode in silence as they entered Warrenton and Coop looked for a place to stop. They passed a church with beautifully carved wooden doors. The parking lot was filled with cars and smoke rose from the chimney.

Riley leaned forward to get a better look. "Why is the parking lot filled with cars that aren't wrecked? It's Sunday. Do you think they're having church?"

Coop put the truck in park. "Unlikely, but possible."

"What better place to gather in a crisis?" Angie asked. "We should check to see if there are people inside. It could be an emergency shelter. They might have food."

Coop was hesitant to enter a crowded church. Angie was desperate not to pass up a perfect opportunity, but after a lively debate, he still wasn't convinced.

Angie unhooked her seatbelt, and said, "Then please just drop me off. I'm willing to risk it."

"We can't let you go alone," Riley said, then laid her hand on Coop's arm. "We don't have to stay, but we should at least look. They could have useful information about what's ahead, at the very least."

Coop eyed her for a moment, then shifted into drive and turned into the parking lot. "On your heads be it. Girls, get down and wait here with the doors locked."

"We know the drill," Julia said, as she pulled a blanket over her head.

Angie got out and walked ahead of Coop and Riley. They

slowly approached the church. There didn't seem to be any sentries in the area. Angie was determined to go into that church even if Coop changed his mind. She caught snippets of the animated discussion going on behind her but tried not to listen. If the church was safe, she'd stay and probably never see Coop and Riley again. Though she was deeply indebted to them, she had to do what was best for herself and her family.

The church doors opened seconds before Angie reached them. A tall, kind-looking man with a shotgun resting on his shoulder stepped out. Angie saw Coop's hand move to his holster. The man stiffened until he noticed Riley and Angie. He lowered the gun and stuck out his enormous hand for Coop to shake.

"Brett Collins. Sorry about the gun, but we never know who we'll be facing when we open the door. Is it just the three of you?"

Coop stared at Mr. Collins's proffered hand for a moment before shaking it without answering his question. "Neal Cooper. We saw the cars in the parking lot and thought we'd stop."

Angie was startled to hear Coop use his real name, Neal, the same as her son. It hadn't occurred to her to ask his real name. It made her feel a strange affinity to him.

Brett checked out their odd attire before saying, "Looks like you've had some trouble, but who hasn't these days? We don't have much. Come in and see what we can do to help."

Coop gave a restrained smile. "That's kind of you."

Riley stepped forward and offered her hand. "Dr. Riley Poole. Please, call me Riley."

Angie caught Coop frowning behind her and couldn't help but smile. He clearly hadn't wanted Brett to know they were doctors. It made her curious about their story. She hoped she'd have the chance to ask.

Brett smiled. "A doctor? Excellent news. We have sick and injured here and can really use your help."

"Coop's a doctor, too," Angie blurted out, and Coop's frown grew exponentially.

Angie saw Riley trying to hide a smile. "This is our new friend, Angie Hughes," she said.

Brett nodded and motioned for them to follow him down a flight of stairs to a large social hall beneath the chapel. The crowd grew quiet when they entered, and fifty pairs of eyes stared back at them.

"We have a few more friends to join us," Brett said. "These are Drs. Neal Cooper and Riley Poole, and their friend Angie Hughes."

The occupants broke into action at once and crowded around them. A woman who looked to be in her mid-twenties took Angie by the arm and led her to a cot.

After handing her a set of white hospital sheets and a blanket, she said, "My name is Rosie Taylor. I'm from Warrenton. I was a schoolteacher before the CME. I'm working on setting up a study schedule. It's been a challenge under the circumstances."

Angie shook her hand, and said, "I commend you for trying." She told her about Allyson, Neal, and Grant. "I hope someone is doing the same for my children back home."

"I'm sure they're fine, Angie. They're with your parents, and we don't even know if the CME hit that far away."

Angie gave her a sad smile. Logic told her that if the CME had only struck locally, help would have arrived days ago. "My one hope is that it didn't."

Rosie nodded. "We have food over at those tables along the back wall. We're rationing, but that tall man with the black hair will explain everything. His name is John."

"Thank you, Rosie. We're starving. The house we were staying in last night burned down. We lost everything and haven't eaten since dinnertime."

"Oh, my lord. You poor things. How did that happen?"

"Just an accident. Spark from the fireplace we think."

"You can never be too careful. Come on, let's get you something to eat."

Rosie started for the table, but Angie stopped when she saw Riley waving to her from the base of the stairs. "I need to talk to Riley. I'll find my way to the food table when I'm done."

Rosie smiled before hurrying off to help someone else. Angie made her way through the crowd to Riley.

"Coop went to bring the girls in," she said. "We're going to eat and rest for a bit, then we're leaving to find our own place to stay. Coop's uneasy about staying here for some reason. I was hoping to talk you into coming with us."

Angie shook her head. "I'm sorry, Riley. I'm deeply grateful for all you've done for me, but I'm staying. I'll rest for a few days and get my strength up before finding a way to get home. I wish you all the best and hope you make it back to your other children someday."

Riley gave her a quick hug, then hurried up the stairs to Coop. Angie was sad to see them go, surprised at how close she felt to them after just a day. She remembered what Riley had said about people bonding quickly in a crisis. It had already happened twice in a week. She wondered how many more friends she'd make before she reached home.

CHAPTER 7

ANGIE PULLED her blanket up under her chin and rested her head on the pillow with a contented sigh. It was the first night she'd felt protected and safe since the crash. She was surrounded by nearly a hundred kind people in a warm, welcoming place. She'd decided to give herself three or four days in Warrenton before searching for a way back to Pennsylvania. As much as she wanted to find an abandoned car with a full tank and strike out on her own, she knew it wasn't worth the risk. Even if waiting delayed her for a week or more, she'd stay until she found others traveling north.

She tucked her hand under her head as she stared at the ceiling, wondering where Coop, Riley, and the girls ended up for the night. Coop's adamant refusal to stay at the church baffled her. He seemed like a rational person, but Angie believed that taking the girls away was reckless. She'd never know where they'd gone or where they'd end up. "I wish you all the best," she whispered, meaning it with all her heart. Those girls had suffered enough for three lifetimes. She forgot about the others she'd met along the way and fell into a deep sleep, imagining the faces of her own beloved children.

Sometime later, a deafening bang followed by an ear-splitting shriek invaded her dreams. As she had the previous night, she bolted to a sitting position and stared round the room in confusion. All she could make out in the dim glow of the exit signs was the flash of gunfire. She dove under her cot and covered her ears with her hands, hoping the shooters hadn't noticed her. She was terrified beyond reason. Her only movement was the uncontrollable trembling of her body.

Within seconds of sliding into her hiding place, someone grabbed her by the arm and dragged her out from under the cot like she weighed no more than a feather. She turned her head just far enough to get a glimpse of the man. He was tall with a large build and was wearing what looked like military camouflage.

He leaned over and rolled her onto her back. "Get up!" he ordered.

Angie scrambled to her feet and raise her arms in surrender. In the pandemonium going on around her, she made out four other men as large as the one who'd pulled her out from under the bed. The others had stopped firing their weapons and were herding their terrified hostages toward the stairs.

Her captor gave her a shove, and growled, "Follow them."

Without a word, Angie got into line behind the others and mounted the stairs. She almost retched at the sight of a baby's body with a bleeding skull. Next to him, a woman who lay face down groaned as Angie passed. A bloodstain was spreading across the back of her pajama top. Angie guessed that she was the baby's mother. Squeezing her eyes closed against the bloody scene, she felt her way up the rest of the steps. Angie didn't open her eyes until she felt freezing air on her face and realized they'd reached the parking lot.

Her captor pointed at a parked van ten feet away. "Get in and keep quiet," he said after giving her another shove.

She stopped at the open van door. "But I need my coat, shoes, and other belongings. I'll freeze to death."

He pointed his rifle at her. "Someone will get them. Shut up and get in."

Angie obeyed and quickly climbed in without daring to question him further. She spotted Rosie huddled in the back seat, staring at her with eyes wide in terror. She dropped onto the seat beside her and took her hand.

Putting her lips close to Rosie's ear, she whispered, "I'm here and I won't leave your side. We'll get each other through this."

Tears dripped onto Rosie's cheeks as she nodded. She squeezed Angie's hand so hard she feared her fingers would break. Angie pulled her hand free and put an arm around her. Rosie rested her head on Angie's shoulder and silently sobbed. Angie did her best to keep her emotions in check. She had to be strong for Rosie.

Once every seat in the ten-passenger van contained a hostage, one of the men climbed into the driver seat and started the engine. When the military-style truck in front of them started moving away, the driver put the truck in gear and followed it out of the parking lot. Angie turned and watched the church growing smaller through the back window as they drove away. She'd fooled herself into thinking she was safe in that place, just as she had in the plane, and the cottage. The hard lesson had finally pushed through her thick skull. None of them were safe anywhere.

"Where are you taking us?" John asked when the driver pulled onto a highway leading out of Warrenton.

A brute of a man in the front passenger seat backhanded him across the cheek. "Shut it. You'll see when we get there."

The driver glared at the man. "You'd better rein it in, Jepson. After what you did to that woman in the church, you're going to have a lot to explain to Director Branson. This wasn't how the operation was supposed to go."

Jepson backed off at hearing that and relaxed against his seat. "Sure, Brooks. You got it."

Brooks glanced at John in the rearview mirror. "We're taking you to our camp in an abandoned scouting facility. We're starting a community. We need skilled workers and more hands to get it up and running."

A middle-aged man Angie didn't recognize leaned forward, and said, "What kind of community murders woman and children, and drags people from their beds in the dead of night to take them hostage?"

Jepson gave him a sneer, but Brooks said, "It wasn't supposed to happen that way. Prospective residents usually come voluntarily. We find them cold and hungry, eager to accept the help we offer. Jepson here is jumpy and lost it when someone refused to go with him."

"He's more than jumpy," the man said. "He's a cowardly, cold-blooded murderer."

Jepson lifted his hand to strike again, but Brooks gave a slight shake of his head, and he lowered his arm. A woman seated next to the man whispered something to him. He crossed his arms and leaned back. Angie blew out the breath she'd been holding in fear that Jepson would kill him right there in the van. Rosie had quieted and was slumped against the seat. She and Angie exchanged looks and kept their mouths shut.

A GRAY DAWN was breaking when Brooks pulled up to a gated chain link fence. When he rolled down his window and poked his head out, two guards, who looked no older than eighteen, slid the gate open to let them through. Brooks drove to a large, olive-green tent and parked the van in front.

Turning to Brooks, he said, "You'd better lay low until I smooth things over with Director Branson."

Jepson jumped out of the van and ducked between two tents.

Angie watched him disappear, thinking that it would be too soon if she ever saw him again.

Brooks got out and opened the van door and told the hostages to exit. As they climbed out, he directed them to the tent door. "Find a seat inside and wait. Someone will come soon and give you a briefing."

Angie took in her surroundings as she followed Rosie toward the tent. The compound reminded her of the set from the TV show *M*A*S*H*. She wondered how their captors had managed to set the place up so fast. Only nine days had passed since the CME. It was early morning, so the only people she saw were guards patrolling the compound. Most of them looked no more than eighteen. Angie wasn't sure if they were friendlies or enemies. She hadn't believed a word of the calm and reasonable spiel Brooks gave about building a welcoming community. The hostages would need to be on their guard.

Rosie held the door open for her to enter the tent first. Rows of wooden tables with benches were lined up in the middle around a wood burning stove. It was clearly the mess hall. The only people inside were the kitchen staff beginning breakfast preparations. Angie had no doubt of where they'd acquired the crates of food stacked along the back wall. Regardless of where it had come from, her stomach growled at the enticing aroma of roasted meat.

She made her way to her companions from the church who were huddled around the stove. She sank onto a bench and held her hands out to warm them. Searching the eyes of her companions told her they were as confused and afraid as she was.

The middle-aged woman she hadn't met kept her gaze glued to the flames as she said, "What is this place? A concentration camp? Has the entire world gone mad?"

The man Angie guessed was her husband put his arm around her. "I'd have to say yes at the moment, Goldie," he said softly.

John wiped his eyes with the back of his hand. "Did you see

what Jepson did to Margret? Shot her right in the back. Killed that baby. If they're capable committing such atrocities, what will they do to us?"

Rosie sat forward and interrupted him. "You heard what that Brooks guy said. Jepson acted on his own."

John stared at her with his anguish filled eyes. "Why should we believe him? We saw those monsters murder innocents right in front of us."

Before Rosie could answer, the door opened, letting in a rush of cold air. Another group of bedraggled people shuffled in and headed toward the stove. They were in rough shape. The members of Angie's group watched them, commiserating with their plight.

A teenage girl was silently staring at Angie. "You just get here too?" When Angie gave her a slight nod, she said, "Can you believe this place? Food, heat, tents. It's awesome."

Angie wrapped her arms around herself and shivered despite the warmth. "Yes, we were just brought here against our wills. Awesome is not what I would call it."

The girl's eyes widened as she sat up straighter. "Seriously? We were freezing and starving to death. These guys saved our lives."

Angie was even more confused than before. Why would Brooks and his thugs have been so violent with the people in the church but kind to the girl's group? None of what was happening made sense.

"We were safe and warm, staying in a church basement with several others. They dragged us out of our beds and forced us to come here. They shot several of our group. Some died," Angie said slowly.

When she stopped speaking, she noticed others of the girl's group staring at her in shock.

"That can't be true," a tall, willowy woman in her thirties said.

John looked her in the eye. "Trust me. It's true."

The new people shared glances before one man who looked to be in charge said, "Thanks for warning us. We'll make sure to be on our guard."

The door swung open again, and a woman with a large build, holding a clipboard strode in. Stepping to the front of the group, she said, "My name is Sabrina Chambers. I'm the human resource director here. Each of you please take a seat facing me and we'll begin the orientation."

Goldie's husband remained standing and crossed his arms. "Are we prisoners or can we leave if we want to? Why were our people murdered?"

"Mr...," Sabrina said and gestured for the man to give his name.

"Rutledge," he answered reluctantly. "Edward Rutledge."

Sabrina scribbled his name on the clipboard. "Mr. Rutledge, on behalf of Director Branson, I apologize for the brutal and senseless loss of life. The parties responsible are being dealt with. That unfortunate incident is not what we're about here."

John stood and took a step toward her. "*Unfortunate incident?* Is that what you call cold blooded murder?" Sabrina kept her eyes on him as she pressed the point of her pen to the clipboard. Before she could ask his name, he blurted, "John Tillman."

Sabrina reached up and massaged her neck while she said, "Forgive me, Mr. Tillman. I was not trying to make light of what happened. As I said, it was brutal and senseless. We're grieved that we can't bring those poor souls back to life. Like so many have been forced to do in the past week, we must move forward."

John glared at her for a moment before shaking his head. "I'm not sure I'll ever be able to move past the murders I witnessed, but I understand you have business to conduct here. First, please answer Edward's questions."

"I appreciate that," Sabrina said. "Prisoner isn't the word I would use, but we can't allow you to leave and risk revealing our location to others. We'd be overrun and we don't have the resources. If you prove cooperative in time, you'll be allowed to leave for brief periods to help with supply runs. Once you see what we have to offer here, you won't want to leave. And honestly, where else would you go?"

John lowered himself onto the bench without a word. Angie could tell he was far from satisfied with her answer. At least they finally knew where they stood.

No one else interrupted as Sabrina explained how the compound operated and what their responsibilities were. Each person would be assigned a tent large enough for four people. In the case of families with young children, they'd be allotted quarters large enough to accommodate all of them. They would all be required to complete a questionnaire outlining any specialized skills or strengths they possessed. Each healthy person was expected to work and contribute to the whole.

What she'd described sounded like a Siberian work camp to Angie. All she wanted was to get home to her children. She couldn't have cared less about the utopian community their director wanted to create. She had no choice but to cooperate. Her hope was that if she were a model prisoner, she'd find a way to escape while out on a supply run. She saw no other way to gain her freedom.

AFTER A BREAKFAST of fried eggs with pork, homemade bread, and canned peaches, she left to find her quarters. She'd be bunking with three other women she'd never met. She asked Sabrina if she could share a tent with Rosie, but her request was denied.

As she and Rosie crossed the open square of the compound, Angie said, "It looks like our tents are close together. I'm sure we'll have time to visit. What job were you assigned to?"

"Laundry tent," she said with a half-grin. "I told Sabrina I'm a teacher. She said they're working on setting up a school. I offered to help with that, so hopefully I won't be a laundress for long. Where were you assigned?"

"Mess hall," she said with a laugh. "When they discover what a rotten cook I am, I'm sure I'll be reassigned too. Maybe I'll rate cleaning the latrines. They don't have much need around her for an art curator."

Rosie snickered at that. "What did you do in the former world?"

"My husband and I own an art gallery. I doubt there will be much call for my particular skill set in this place."

"Probably not. I'll see if I can get you on as the art teacher once the school is up and running."

I won't be here that long, Angie thought but kept that to herself as they walked. They reached her tent before Rosie's, so Angie gave her a warm hug, then waited at the tent door, watching Rosie until she reached her assigned quarters. Before entering her tent, Angie leaned her ear to the canvas wall and caught snippets of conversation between the women who would be her roommates.

"Living here hasn't been what I expected," one of them with a younger sounding voice said.

"It's not, but it's better than the alternative," one with an older and more authoritative voice said.

"Is it?" the first woman said.

Angie heard what sounded like one of them getting up and moving in the tent. "Don't talk like that," a third woman said. "We were freezing and starving. I wouldn't call these people our saviors, but we are alive. Make the best of it while we regain our strength. Our situation may improve as more people are brought here."

Angie cleared her throat as she opened the door and ducked inside. Once her eyes adjusted to the darkness, she saw a woman in her early twenties sitting on a cot beside a thirtyish woman with shoulder length, brown curly hair that could have used a brush. The third woman lying in a sleeping bag on her cot was closer to Angie's age. She wore a knit cap, but wisps of her gray streaked hair stuck out around the edges. None of them looked pleased to see her. Angie instantly felt like an intruder.

She dropped her sleeping bag and other personal items her captors had placed on the empty cot near the door, then introduced herself. "I'm your new bunkmate."

The one lying on the cot eyed her with suspicion for a moment before unzipping her sleeping bag and swinging her bare feet to the floor. "Welcome, Angie. I'm Patricia. The young one there is Maisy. The other is Anna."

Angie gave each a nod. "Hello."

Patricia stood and stretched. "Looks like you've had a rough time of it. Like the rest of us."

Angie lowered her gaze and studied the stained sneakers they'd just given her. "You can't imagine," she whispered.

Maisy stood and placed a hand on Angie's arm. "I bet we can."

Angie looked up and studied the young woman's face. Dark circles rimmed her lovely green eyes, and Angie read trauma there. Her straight blond hair was pulled back from her oval face in messy braids.

Angie put her hand over Maisy's and squeezed. "Yes, I think you might." Turning to the others, she said, "Once we've gotten to know each other better, we'll share our stories. For now, I hope you won't mind answering a few of my questions."

"Be happy to if we can," Anna said.

When Maisy moved to a folding camp chair in the corner, Angie sank onto her cot with a groan. "I appreciate that. What is this place? How long have you been here? How did you get here?"

Patricia crossed her arms and let out a sigh. "This was a Boy Scout encampment. From what we've heard, the man who appointed himself the leader here stumbled on the camp after his house burned down. From what we've heard, he got the idea to bring in other destitute people and start a community. At some point, he got full of himself and turned into a heartless dictator. He insists on being called *Director Branson*. Ludicrous."

"I've heard about that," Angie said. "Why hasn't anyone stood up to him?"

Anna shook her head. "Because he made one ingenious move. Before the rest of us knew what was happening, he armed residents willing to kiss his ass for special treatment. Those of us who refused are treated like prisoners. There's nothing we can do because he knows we're at his mercy. Most of his followers are the worst kind of thugs. Some only go along out of self-preservation. A couple have been to prison."

Maisy leaned forward and whispered, "Branson comes off all humble and ordinary. Acts like he cares about us. Don't be fooled, Angie. The guy's an absolute psychopath."

"I'll keep that in mind."

Patricia rubbed her face before glancing up at Angie. "Five days after the CME, some of Branson's lackeys found our group of twenty from the same small town, walking along the highway in search of food and a warm place to stay. We were elated, seeing them as benevolent rescuers. They gave us food and warmth, but it came at a high price."

Before Angie could ask the rest of the questions swirling in her brain, a recorded bell sound blared through loudspeakers across the camp. Her three bunkmates jumped to their feet in unison and began tidying their cots and personal areas.

"That's our lovely morning wake up call," Anna said as she pulled her hair into a ponytail. "Time to get breakfast before going to work. Where did they assign you?"

"Mess hall. I'm not sure what I'll be doing there," Angie said as she watched them scurrying about like guilty teenagers.

"I work there, too. Second shift," Maisy said while pulling a hoodie over her head. "I'll show you the ropes."

Angie nodded as she began unpacking her provisions. "I've eaten. I'll get settled, then come find you."

Maisy flashed her a friendly smile before following Anna and Patricia out of the tent. Angie was relieved that her roomies had accepted her into their circle so easily.

Once she was alone, Angie stretched out on her cot without even bothering to take off her shoes. It was the first moment alone she'd had since going into the woods to use the bucket on the morning after the fire with Riley, Coop and the gang. She missed them already. After doing a quick calculation, she realized only twenty-four hours had passed since then. As her brain struggled to comprehend it, she asked herself how that was possible. It felt more like a week.

Recalling her tearful goodbye with Riley and the girls reminded her that she'd made such a tragic mistake in staying at the church. Coop's premonition had proved right. What she would have given to be with them at that moment, even if they were traveling in the wrong direction. She still would have been worlds better off. But it was too late. She'd made her bed and was now lying in it.

She sat up and finished unpacking her meager provisions. The man who'd dragged her from the church promised they'd get her belongings. That had been an outright lie, but what could she expect from murderers? It wasn't as if it mattered to her that she'd lost her belongings in the church. What little she'd salvaged from the plane had been destroyed in the cottage fire. For the first time in her living memory, she owned nothing of value. It was a small thing compared to the nightmare she was living, but that realization saddened her.

A knock on the tent door's wooden frame startled her out of her thoughts. "Yes," she called out.

Sabrina swung the door open and strode in with her hands on

her hips. "Why haven't you reported to the mess, Hughes? Your shift supervisor is getting impatient waiting to begin your training. You're off to a poor start."

Angie was too far gone to be intimidated by this woman with no true authority over her. She squared her shoulders and looked her in the eyes. "If my supervisor wanted me to report at a certain time, it would have been a good idea to tell me."

"Show me your orientation sheet." Angie grabbed the paper off the cot and thrust it at Sabrina. She scanned it for a moment, then handed it back to Angie. "A slight oversight. I'll see it doesn't happen again. Finish what you were doing, then report to Elaine."

When she turned to leave, Angie said, "Don't you have anything else you'd like to say?"

Sabrina spun around to face her. "Such as?"

"An apology. You came in here accusing me of...what? Insubordination? Disobedience? Just because the world's gone to hell doesn't mean common courtesy has died. There's no reason to be rude. Unless you've always been uncivil."

Sabrina glared at Angie for a moment before softening her defensive posture. "You're absolutely right. I never would have treated anyone this way before the CME. We've all been bossing each other so much it's become second nature. You have my apologies, Mrs. Hughes."

Angie extended her hand. "Call me Angie."

Sabrina hesitated before taking Angie's hand, then gave it a firm shake before letting go and hurrying toward the door. She stopped before going out and gave Angie a look of respect and gratitude.

"Thanks for the reminder, Angie. A little humanity goes a long way."

"Something we can all use a lot more of right now." Sabrina dipped her head and left without another word. "Score one for me," Angie whispered, then finished her unpacking and headed for the mess hall.

The exchange with Sabrina had been a good reminder for her too. It was all too easy to put up walls in self-defense, but they were all the same people they'd been before the disaster. Or had the new reality changed everything? She resolved to go out of her way to lighten burdens and make life a little brighter for the people she interacted with. Even if it didn't set off a positive chain reaction, it certainly couldn't make life any worse.

CHAPTER 8

ANGIE MASSAGED her neck as she left the dining tent at the end of her shift. Two weeks had passed since the incident at the church, but she was no closer to finding a way to break free and make it home to her children. Each day passed exactly as the one before. The only exception to the daily routine was on mornings when Branson's minions showed up with vans of new arrivals. A few of the more desperate ones had come by choice but most had been dragged to the camp against their wills like Angie. They soon would learn as she had that their chances of escape were slim to impossible.

Angie went through the motions of her day, keeping her head down, doing whatever it took to avoid drawing attention to herself. The one indulgence she allowed herself was a nightly walk of the compound's perimeter fence. On her first night in camp, she'd been less than thrilled to discover that Patricia snored like a lumberjack. Anna and Maisy managed to slumber blissfully through the din, but Angie didn't catch a moment's rest.

Getting sufficient sleep was vital to maintaining her physical health and an alert mental state, so Angie started her nightly walks in the hope of exhausting herself enough to sleep through Patricia's snoring. Her ploy served another purpose. It gave her a chance to become familiar with the layout of the compound. After the first week, the guards grew used to seeing her nightly jaunts and paid no attention to her. She knew that could come in handy when her time came to attempt an escape.

She slowly pulled the flap open when she reached the tent and was relieved to find it empty. Such moments of solitude were rare in the crowded camp. She dropped onto her cot, boots and all, and covered her eyes with her arm. After taking a few deep breaths, she felt the tension begin to drain from her body, hoping for a half hour of peace before going to shower and eat her meager dinner at the fire pit.

While working in the mess hall, Angie had soon learned of the cruel inequalities that existed between Branson's goons and the rest of the camp's *residents*. Members of Branson's staff were fed from plates piled high with steaming food while the captives were given thin soup or rice with crusts of bread, which caused the residents to lose weight and be malnourished. To avoid the torture of seeing and smelling the food they were denied, the hostages ate at the fire pit instead of inside in the warm mess tent.

As a member of the kitchen staff, Angie knew all too well that Branson had more than enough stores to feed everyone equally in the camp. But withholding food was one of The Director's strategies to force people over to his side and sign their lives over to him.

Each night, Angie counted fewer people at the fire pit and more at the tables in the mess tent. The ones who remained outside refused to bow to Branson's will like Angie, but she feared that over time, they'd all be forced to relent or face starvation. It is the worst kind of torture, especially since most of the so-called residents had never known a day of hunger in their lives. Stealing food could bring a beating from Branson's goons.

Angie felt the outline of her ribs beneath her sweater, then shook her head to clear it. "Stop predicting your doom. You haven't starved yet."

"I'm glad to hear that," Patricia said as she ducked into the tent. She laughed as she tossed her pack in a corner. "Do I need to worry that you've started talking to yourself?"

Angie sat up and stared at the floor to hide her blushing cheeks. "Thought I was alone," she mumbled.

"No worries. We all do it. Have you eaten?"

Angie got to her feet and reached for her own pack. "Not yet. I was trying to talk myself into going for a shower before dinner."

"I'll wait for you. Swing by on your way back, and I'll join you for our *sumptuous* feast."

Angie gave her a quick nod as she passed on her way out. Going to dinner with Patricia meant she'd have to cut her shower short, but she still permitted herself ten minutes under the glorious warm water, which was five minutes longer than residents were allowed. She was alone in the shower room and figured it was worth the risk of going over her allotted time. It was one of her small ways of sticking it to Branson.

She dressed quickly after drying off, then hurried by to pick up Patricia. Maisy was with her in the tent, so she joined them at the fire pit after they got their rations from the mess hall. There was a crowd close to the fire, so the three of them found empty logs out of the reach of the warm flames. It was her fault for taking so long in the showers, but she still considered it worth it.

She was lowering herself onto the log when two guards passed, dragging a third man between them. She set her plate down and pushed through the crowd to get a clearer view of what was happening. The guards dropped the man on the ground and one of them gave him a kick in the ribs before turning to the shocked crowd.

Pointing to the man lying in a patch of snow, the guard said, "Let me introduce Dr. Adrian Landry, the man responsible for withholding vital information from the world on how devastating the CME would be. Director Branson wants him alive to suffer. None of you are to lay a hand on him or help him in any way."

A tall middle-aged man named David stepped closer to the guard. "What are you talking about? The government warned us about the CME. I thought it just came earlier than they predicted."

Dr. Landry rolled over, then groaned and grabbed his side as he pushed himself to a sitting position. Angie was shocked at the sight of him. He was fortyish looking and balding, with a slight build. He looked like he was on the verge of starvation, but the most startling thing about his appearance was the bruises and cuts on his face and upper body. The guards had been meticulous in following Branson's orders to beat but not kill the man.

Dr. Landry lifted the hem of his button-down shirt to his face and dabbed at his cuts for a moment before raising his eyes to the stunned crowd.

"What this man says is true. I was an astrophysicist at the Goddard Space Center just outside Washington, DC. I was the one who discovered a second CME heading toward earth. It was much bigger and was due to hit before the smaller one you'd been warned about. I told Vice President Kearns of my discovery, but she refused to alert the public. I should have found a way to make the announcement on my own, but I took the coward's way out and did nothing but warn my family. I deserve what these men have done to me and more."

As the import of Dr. Landry's speech sunk in, the strength drained from Angie's legs, and she sank to her knees. If she and Grant had known about the other CME, they wouldn't have left home. They wouldn't have boarded that plane. Grant would be alive, and they'd be safe with their children at home. It was more than her brain and heart could process. Dr. Landry had destroyed her life and possibly been the cause of millions of deaths. He deserved more than a beating. He deserved a firing squad.

One of the guards wound a rope around his wrist, then wrapped it around the tree. "Your new home," he said, then strode off cackling with the other guard.

Dr. Landry slumped against the tree and broke into sobs. Angie's heart softened slightly at witnessing the pathetic figure, but only a little. She knew he deserved every minute of this cruel treatment. She would never bring herself to forgive the man.

Maisy put her hands on her hips and stomped her foot. "I don't care what that man did, he doesn't deserve a beating. That's not how we do things in America. Do we throw away rule of law and all we stand for just because of a catastrophic natural disaster? He's entitled to a trial and due process. And who put Branson in charge? I didn't vote for him. He's nothing more than a petty dictator."

Patricia got up and put her arm around Maisy's shoulders. "I don't disagree, dear, but you better watch what you say. Come on, let's go eat in our tent. Can you walk, Angie?"

She got to her feet and retrieved her plate before following her roommates back to their tent. What Maisy had said made perfect sense. Similar thoughts had crossed Angie's mind since the disaster. The structure of their society had vanished in the aftermath of the CME. The problem for their group was, how could they overthrow Branson and reinstate old laws and practices? Stage a revolution? A coup? If that were possible, the hostages would have already attempted it. Despite her longing for a return to the laws that governed America, she wasn't convinced Dr. Landry was entitled to a fair judgment. He'd plainly admitted his guilt.

Those questions were too overwhelming for Angie to answer in her current state. She ate her meal in silence while Maisy and Patricia filled Anna in on what had happened at the fire pit. She was as stunned by the news as the rest had been. While the three of them droned on about what it all meant, Angie climbed into her sleeping bag and turned toward the wall. Once again, the seams of her fragile existence had been ripped to shreds, and it was more than she could process. She closed her mind to all thoughts except for those of her children.

When the others grew quiet, she pulled on her boots and went for her nightly sojourn along the perimeter of the camp, but it offered no comfort. She returned to the tent as troubled as she'd been when she left and spent the remainder of the night wide awake, waiting for the light of dawn.

ANGIE WENT through the motions of the following day in a haze, numb from lack of sleep, food, and a loss of hope. As she scooped spoonfuls of slop into countless bowls, she avoided the gaze of people who were no more than ghosts to her. Thoughts played on a loop in her mind. *This is the end. What's the point? It's hopeless.* She'd been tempted to relent to Branson's games more than once when she served the overflowing plates of food to his staff. Signing the contract would instantly entitle her to the perks they enjoyed.

Too weary to carry on the endless debate in her mind, she resolved to request a meeting with Branson at the end of the lunch service. As she was removing her apron, the two guards from the previous day dragged Dr. Landry into the mess hall and forced him onto a bench. His hands were still tied, and his bruises had darkened. The guards were constantly slapping and kicking him. Angie was surprised at her relief that he'd survived when she'd wished for his death a day earlier. Branson must have meant it when he said he wanted Landry to suffer.

When one of the guards approached to obtain food for Landry, Angie asked what she should put on his plate.

"The worst you have for that creature. Just enough to keep him breathing," he answered with a sneer.

Angie filled a bowl with the indecipherable mush they'd been given for lunch and held it out to him. He grabbed it from her and dumped half on the floor.

She scowled at him, and said, "I'll have to clean that up, and what would Director Branson think of you wasting food? I could have poured the extra back into the pot."

He gave her a shrug before dropping Landry's bowl onto the table in front of him, then joining his comrades on the other side of the mess hall. After cleaning up the spilled food, Angie watched Landry trying to eat with his hands tied and felt a tinge of compassion for him. While the guards were distracted, she loosened his restraints, and refilled his bowl.

As he stared at her in confusion, she leaned close to him, and whispered, "This doesn't mean I forgive you, but no one deserves this kind of treatment."

Landry lifted his spoon but stopped before scooping up his food. "Don't forgive me. I don't deserve it. But thank you for your kindness."

She walked away from him without another word passing between them. When she was done with her duties, instead of using her break to go see Branson as she had resolved, she took her bowl of slop to Landry's table and sat across from him. Her internal debate was decided. She would never acquiesce to the man who could deliberately withhold food from people, allow others to treat women as playthings, and handle Landry in such a barbaric manner. No matter what she'd have to face in the future, Angie couldn't allow herself to become the captors she loathed. She'd cling to her last remnants of humanity, whatever the cost.

With her resolve renewed, Angie's day flew by. She'd stumbled around in the gloom since arriving at the camp. It was a relief to feel the darkness lifting despite the constant gnawing hunger. She couldn't change her circumstances, but she could control her reaction to them. She smiled at the residents as she served them and even offered the occasional encouraging word. They were all struggling and needed their spirits lifted.

As she ate her dinner at the fire pit and chatted with the people seated around her that evening, her ears perked up when she heard a voice that sounded like Riley Poole. Angie paused to listen to the conversation before stepping out of the shadows. She caught the words *'shot Julia'*. Riley was asking for blood donors for a transfusion. Angie had figured that Riley, Coop, and Julia were hundreds of miles away in southern Virginia by then. How had they gotten captured? Who'd shot Julia?

Riley was speaking to a man named Marcus who volunteered to donate blood. He pulled Riley into a hug as others came forward with offers to donate as well.

Angie stepped into the firelight, and said, "I'll donate if I'm compatible."

Riley's eyes widened in recognition. "Angie!" she cried and threw her arms around her friend. "We thought you were dead. We went to the church, but no one knew what happened to you."

Angie stepped away and wiped her eyes. "Mystery solved. I've been a hostage here since that horrible night. So, one of these monsters shot Julia? Let me guess, Jepson? He has a reputation around here for being trigger happy."

"He's the one. He shot her in the leg. We were able to repair the damage, but she's lost a lot of blood and needs a transfusion. Do you know your type?"

"I think I'm O-positive, but I'm not sure."

Coop came up behind Riley and gave Angie a tight hug when he recognized her. "Angie, thank God," he said, then stepped away and shook his head at Riley. "They used the last of the supply of testing kits two days ago. We need to get our hands on one."

"Our benevolent jailers might have what you need," a man called from behind Riley.

She spun around to face Dr. Landry slumped against the tree he was tied to. He was wrapped in a thin blanket and visibly shivering.

"Who's that and why is he tied to a tree like a dog?" Riley asked as she started for him.

Marcus put his hand out to stop her. "Leave him be." He cocked his head toward the mess tent. "That bunch won't like it if you help him."

"Why? What did he do?" Coop asked.

"That's Dr. Adrian Landry," Angie said. "He knew hell was about to rain down on us but didn't alert the public. Our captors weren't too happy to hear that. They beat him nearly to death."

Riley walked past Marcus' outstretched arm and grabbed two blankets from one of the camp chairs. "Another doctor? We can use him. I don't care what he's done."

Angie didn't join Riley when she approached Dr. Landry and sat across from him on the frozen ground. She admired Riley's courage and compassion. Coop followed Riley and helped her get Dr. Landry to his feet. No one tried to stop them when they walked him to the infirmary. Angie wished she could go with them but decided to give the doctors their space to treat Landry's injuries. She finished her meal in silence, then stayed at the fire pit hoping Riley or Coop would return but they never did. After waiting as long as she could, she went to her tent and submitted herself to her nightly bout of insomnia.

ANGIE WOKE with a start just before dawn. She'd planned to sneak out and look for Coop and Riley after her tent-mates were asleep, but she'd drifted off and slept through the night. It was the first time Patricia's snoring hadn't disturbed her sleep, and Angie was at a loss to explain why. She was just grateful, and hoped it was a sign of future peaceful nights to come.

She lay in the fading dark staring at the tent roof as events of the past two days ran through her mind. As brokenhearted as Angie was that Julia had been shot and her friends captured, she was glad to know they were still alive. It was comforting to have people in camp who she trusted and felt a connection to. She hoped once Julia was recovered, the four of them could escape together.

The buzz at the campfire had been all about Riley and Coop. Having two skilled surgeons on staff was a major boon. The only medical professionals they had in camp to that point were a few nurses, a dentist, an Army medic, and a psychologist. Disease and injuries plagued the camp, and those few health professionals did their best they could to combat them, but Riley and Coop had skills on a whole other level. Angie was certain Branson had already conscripted them into running the infirmary.

The other major topic of conversation the night before had been about Jepson shooting Julia. Angie heard rumors that after the murders Jepson committed at the church and then shooting Julia, Branson cut off one of Jepson's fingers as punishment and to make him an example to the other guards. It made her wonder what kind of man Branson had been before the CME, and what he'd done for a living.

Angie had only seen Branson three times since arriving in camp and had never spoken to him. She weirdly hoped he'd always been an odious human being. Was he an evil person before the CME or did the CME make him become evil? If his behavior changed after the CME, it meant anyone could be capable of such a drastic change for the worse. It was hard to remain an honorable person when so much had changed. It seemed like the rules of life had shifted unalterably.

She thought of the people she'd met since the disaster and was comforted that most still had good hearts despite the terrors happening around them. Isaac had saved her on the road to town after the crash. Dr. Hamilton had given her medicines and hope, even if Kyle had died in the end. Coop and Riley stopped for her and took her along. It wasn't their fault she'd made the tragically wrong choice to stay at the church. They'd tried to talk her into leaving with them. She wondered if they might have avoided Branson's men with her help.

Recalling these events reminded her of Hannah. In all the commotion the previous night, Angie hadn't thought to ask about her, and Coop and Riley hadn't brought up her name. Angie threw on her dirty clothes from the previous day, then hurried out to look for Riley. She couldn't wait any longer to hear what happened to them since they parted ways. As she rushed across the compound, she bumped into a woman she hadn't noticed in the dim light. As the woman struggled to regain her balance, she turned and glared at Angie.

The look on her face was so comical that Angie burst out laughing. "I'm sorry, Riley. I was going to look for you and nearly bowled you over in the process. Are you hurt?"

Riley smiled and shook her head. "Just startled. What's the rush? It doesn't look like we're going anywhere soon."

Angie took Riley by the arm and led her to the fire pit containing a few dying embers. "I'll get the fire going and we can talk. No one will be out here for at least another hour."

Riley checked the surrounding area before going with her. "Will the guards catch us?"

Angie shook her head, then picked up some twigs and pine needles from a pile beside the pit and tossed them onto the coals.

"We're allowed to be here. No one will notice us anyway." Once the fire was roaring, she sat beside Riley and held her hands out to the flames. "I have a million questions, but first, why isn't Hannah with you? No one has mentioned her. Did you leave her with another family?"

Riley's shoulders slumped and she became quiet. She began wiping at the tears trickling down her cheeks. "I've been dreading that question. We lost Hannah about a week ago. It's a long, complicated story that leads to why Julia was shot and how we were captured. I promise to tell you everything someday, but I'm exhausted and my emotions are still too raw. We've been through such a nightmare that it makes the cottage burning down feel like child's play. You probably wouldn't believe me." She stopped and looked into Angie's eyes. "What am I saying? Of course, the woman who survived a plane crash would believe me."

"After everything we've all endured, nothing is unbelievable anymore." She grew quiet for a moment, then said, "I'm so sorry about Hannah. She was a sweet girl. At least she's reunited with her parents."

"We've been telling ourselves that but it's small comfort. I want to believe it's true, I'm focused on getting Julia well so we can find a way out of this place."

"You mean escape? I've been planning to make a break for it too, but I'm losing hope that it's possible."

"We're willing to do whatever it takes." She paused, then threw a rock at the now blazing fire. *"Whatever it takes."*

Angie reached for her hand and cradled it in hers. "I can't tell you how happy I am to hear that. Are the rumors about Jepson true? Did Branson cut off his finger?"

Riley gave an almost imperceptible nod. "Right in front of Coop. Then, he ordered him to treat the man's wound. Coop had to treat the man who shot my daughter! I feel like we're living in some cheap horror flick."

Angie leaned closer, and whispered, "Did he do it? Did Coop treat Jepson?" Riley gave another nod. "I don't even know how to process that. All I can do is say how sorry I am. I know that doesn't help."

"I appreciate you saying it though. We treated Dr. Landry's injuries, too. Branson wasn't too thrilled with that, but he didn't punish us. Landry will survive. He told me his whole sordid story. Do you know him well?"

She let out her breath as she shook her head. "I've only known of his existence for two days." She looked away as she said, "I wanted him dead after I heard what he'd done. But not anymore. I'm not excusing or forgiving him, but I'm appalled at the way he's been treated here."

Riley poked at the fire with a stick for a moment before tossing it into the flames. "I've witnessed that firsthand. He's lucky to be alive. If Coop and I hadn't shown up when we did, he wouldn't have lasted another day."

"I've come to pity him slightly," Angie reluctantly admitted. "How can any of us say how we would have acted in his place? Defying the Vice President would have meant standing up to one of the most powerful people in the world. I don't know if I would have had the courage to do that."

"Good point. All I can say is that I hope I would have made a better choice."

Not wanting to waste her few precious moments alone with Riley talking about Dr. Landry, Angie abruptly changed the subject. "How's Julia? Did you find any donors? Did she get the transfusion?"

She noticed the slight hesitation before Riley said, "She did, and her condition is much improved."

"That's great news. Why the sad face? What aren't you telling me?"

Riley pulled her curly red hair into a ponytail before answering. Angie recognized that she was stalling. It just piqued her curiosity more.

"It's nothing," Riley finally said. "Silly really. The blood donor was Branson. He's the monster who saved my daughter's life. Between the Jepson incident and this, my emotions are careening all over the place."

Angie gave a quiet whistle. "I don't blame you. I'm shocked that Branson was even willing to donate."

"Coop and I were too, but he was the only person sure of his O-neg blood type. I was tempted to refuse his offer, but Julia's life was at stake. It shouldn't matter who the donation comes from, but I can't shake my distaste at having that man's blood running through my daughter's body."

"You have to let it go, Riley. Focus on the fact that Julia will survive. As a mother, I understand that nothing is more important than your child's wellbeing. Be careful, though. Branson will expect something in return."

Riley got to her feet and stretched. "I'm doing my best to let it go, but it still creeps me out. I'm sure you're right about Branson. I'm on my way to get Julia the heaping plate of pancakes she requested, then I need to do my rounds. I'll look for you later."

"My shift in the mess hall ends at five. I'll find you." As Riley turned to go, Angie grabbed hold of her hand to stop her. "I'm truly sorry you didn't make it to your uncle's ranch, but I'm grateful to be reunited with friends."

"And we're thrilled to have found out you survived. We'll make it to the ranch. You'll get home to your family. You have my promise."

Angie watched until Riley entered the mess hall before going back to her tent to get ready for the day. Though her current life was foreign in so many ways, she was grateful for the one thing that hadn't changed. People were still people. Most were made from good stock and the Bransons of the world were rare. She needed that hope to cling to as she adjusted to her new life.

CHAPTER 9

ANGIE DIDN'T GET a chance to visit Julia until her afternoon break. She pushed aside the canvas wall separating Julia's room from the rest of the infirmary and was delighted when Julia's face brightened at seeing her.

"Angie, you're alive!" she cried as Angie stepped into her room. "How did you get here?" A woman Angie guessed to be a nurse moved between her and Julia, but Julia waved her off. "It's safe, Dashay. Angie's my friend."

Dashay was an early thirtyish, gorgeous Black woman with the most dazzling smile Angie had ever seen. Her hair was arranged in intricate braids, and she was dressed in clean, stylish clothes. She looked nothing like she was surviving in an apocalypse. Angie glanced down at her clothes which were rumpled, smudged with dirt and a size too big for her. She was at a complete loss as to how Dashay had managed to look so amazing. She was tempted to ask, but she was there for Julia, not to compare stories with Dashay.

Angie sat on the edge of the bed and took Julia's hand. "I was taken hostage at the church. Coop and your mom told me about your ordeal. I got off easy. I'm so sorry about Hannah. She was such a sweet girl."

Tears welled up in Julia's eyes. "It was so horrible. The worst day of my whole life except when Dad died. It still doesn't seem real that she's gone."

Angie brushed a tear from Julia's chin. "I feel that way about my husband sometimes and wish it was all just a nightmare I could wake up from. Glad we didn't lose you. How are you feeling today?"

Julia beamed at her. "Better now that I know you're alive. My leg hurts pretty bad, but I have the best doctors in the world."

"That's true," Dashay said. "Your mom's an amazing person, Julia. She never left your side those first two days."

Julia nodded. "Coop told me. I never knew how awesome my mom was before the CME. Coop's pretty great, too. I'm lucky." She turned to Angie and said, "What's this place like?"

"If we have to be hostages, the compound's as good a place as any, I suppose. It's safer than on the road, as you know."

"I was scared all the time. I hope Mom lets us stay here until my leg's better."

"Leaving may not be up to her," Dashay said. "We're all trapped here, remember?"

Julia nodded. "I keep forgetting. The pain meds make me dopey."

Angie kissed Julia's cheek and stood to go. "I'm on kitchen detail, like I know how to cook. I'll come back after my shift. Get some rest."

"I will. It'll be easier knowing you're here. Thanks for visiting me."

Angie smiled and gave a quick wave as she left. Before she was out of earshot, she heard Dashay say, "Guess I need to hear her story."

"We have lots of unbelievable stories, but Angie's is pretty incredible" Julia said. "She was the only survivor of a plane crash."

Angie pondered on Julia's comment as she headed back to the mess hall. They all did have incredible stories. Hers hadn't seemed more extraordinary than anyone else's until she looked at it from Julia's perspective.

"I was the sole survivor of a plane crash," she whispered to herself as she walked. "How many people have lived to say that?"

"Angie," she heard a man call, drawing her out of her thoughts. She looked up to see Coop hurrying towards her.

"I'm under orders to bring you to Riley's tent," he said with a laugh. "She has some big announcement for us."

"I'm on my break and just went to visit Julia. I suppose I can spare a few minutes if Riley hurries."

He nodded and turned to lead her to Riley's tent. "She'll appreciate you visiting Julia. Poor girl's been to hell and back."

"She's remarkable for her age. Losing Hannah must have been a devastating blow after everything she'd been through."

"It was for all of us. It hit Riley the hardest." He grew quiet and ran his hand through his hair. "I'd rather not rehash it right now."

"Must have been indescribably awful if neither of you will talk about it. I understand that." She told Coop of her conversation with Riley at the fire pit. "Guess I'll have to be patient to hear what happened."

"We'll fill in the details when the time is right. I want to hear what's happened with you since we parted ways at the church."

"Not much more to tell," she said as Riley rushed into the tent.

Coop and Angie sat on a cot facing Riley, eagerly anticipating her big news.

"How can what you have to tell us be more life-altering than what we've already been through?" Coop asked.

Riley dropped into a lawn chair across from them. "Not *life-altering*. I said *earth-shattering*. The world has ended."

Angie leaned back and crossed her arms. "Yeah, we noticed. Cut to the chase. I have to get back to the kitchen."

Riley leaned closer. "No, I mean, the CME struck the entire planet. It's not localized to this area. Adrian estimates that one year after the event there will only be two or three billion people left alive on the planet. He claims millions in the US alone have already perished."

Angie sprang to her feet. "The entire Earth? They said that wasn't possible."

Riley huffed. "Turns out it is, and it gets worse. Power is out everywhere and won't be back on for years, if ever. Adrian's exact words. *If ever*. No help is coming. This disaster is impacting our families and friends. Everyone we know."

Angie swayed for a moment before lowering herself back onto the cot. "If that's true, my family may be dead. It's even colder in Pennsylvania than here. I have to get out of this blasted place."

Coop squeezed her hand. "We've all got to get out of here. That guy's a lunatic and this place is a circus. I predict it'll only get worse. We'll help break you out, Angie, but you're on your own once we're free. We're still heading south."

Angie flinched when Riley slapped her thigh to get their attention. "Yes, we have to escape, but you're ignoring the big picture. The world has been thrust back to the pre-industrial eighteen hundreds. That means no medication production. No vaccines. No antibiotics. Worse, it means no food processing plants, heat, or fuel production. Once the gas runs out, that's it. No more cars. We won't even have clean water without wells, and most of those function on electric pumps."

Coop ran his hand through his hair. "I've only focused on surviving until the rest of the world could step in to help. This means there is no help and we're all starting from scratch."

Riley fell back in the chair and closed her eyes. "It's been generations since humans lived without electricity. How will we survive?"

Coop got up and peeked through the tent flap to make sure no one was listening. "As devastating as this is, it doesn't change our immediate dilemma. How are we going to get out of the compound with Julia?"

"I might have a solution," Riley said. "You're not going to like it, Coop, but it's our best shot. Branson wants me to go on a med supply run with Brooks tomorrow. I'll find a way to take Brooks out while we're gone and come back with the truck after dark. In the meantime, gather supplies and find an unguarded area along the fence. We'll sneak our stuff and Julia out before anyone knows we're gone."

Coop glared at her. "Are you insane? Take Brooks out? He's twice your size. Are you planning to kill him?"

"Of course not. I'll knock him out or drug him."

Angie stared at her in shock. "Are you insane? We can't let you do that, Riley. It's too dangerous."

"I'll persuade Branson to let me go, instead," Coop said.

"That might alert Branson or make him suspicious. And he's not the type to change his mind. It has to be me."

Coop let out a weary sigh. "Branson's not the only one who never changes their mind."

Riley rested her hand on his shoulder. "Brooks seems to like me, and he helped us with Julia. Coop, figure out how to get Julia out of the infirmary without raising any alarm bells."

Coop put his hand over hers. "How will you know where to meet us? I can't exactly text you."

Angie stood and smoothed her pant legs. "I can help with that. I'm in a tent with three other women. One of them snores, and I'm having trouble sleeping since...events. I know the perimeter area like the back of my hand"

Coop got up and put an arm around her shoulder. "Forgive me

for forgetting you lost your husband. I know that's made all of this many times worse for you."

Angie pulled away and gave a quick nod. "Thanks, Coop. It's been a hell of a time for all of us, but back to what I was saying. I've been taking walks at night, so the guards are used to seeing me wandering around the camp. There's a long stretch of fence at the far east side that no one patrols. It's heavily wooded, and the access road doesn't reach that far. It'll be a hike to get Julia and the supplies to the truck, but no one will see us. For now, I'd better get back before they miss me. I've been gone too long as it is."

"Right," Coop said. "Let's meet at that stretch of fence tonight around three tonight to scope it out."

Angie hugged Riley and hurried out of the tent, trying to appear nonchalant as she walked to the mess hall. Riley's plan was outrageous, but their only chance of escaping the compound was to do something drastic. Angie just hoped she'd find the courage when the time came.

<hr>

ANGIE WAS a twitchy mess for the rest of the day.

When she nearly dropped a plate for the third time at dinner, Patricia said, "What's up with you tonight? You were a sullen lump yesterday and back to your normal self after lunch. Now, you look like you're about to jump out of your skin."

Angie calmed herself by taking a few slow breaths. She had to act normal to keep from arousing suspicion. She'd also been feeling guilty at not being able to let her roommates in on their escape plan. They'd been so kind to her and didn't deserve to be abandoned, but it was impossible to save the whole camp. Angie secretly hoped that she, Coop, and Riley would be able to round up help to liberate the rest of the captives once the four of them were free. It was a long shot, but there had to be a community nearby willing to help the souls trapped in the camp.

"It has nothing to do with the cowardly doctor," she said to Patricia. "It's just been an emotional time for me the past few days. I'm worried about my friend's daughter, and I was thinking about Branson cutting off Jepson's finger. It still creeps me out."

Anna smiled at that. "I think you're safe as long as you don't go shooting anyone."

Angie laughed. "I'll do my best."

The conversation shifted to other topics, but Angie heard little of what they were saying. She did her best to appear calm, but her insides were churning. She hoped she'd be more relaxed after the dry run later that night.

She didn't bother to try to sleep before the rendezvous. She waited until two before dressing in her darkest clothes and sneaking out of the tent. She first made her way to the tool shed. Her supervisor sent her there during the dinner shift to get a wrench to tighten a pipe on the kitchen sink. While she was searching for the wrench, she spotted heavy-duty cutters hanging on the far wall. She'd left the shed unlocked when she went back to the kitchen and hoped no one had locked it behind her. The bolt cutters would make breaking through the chain-link fence much easier.

She was relieved to find the shed unlocked when she reached it and hoped fate was finally working in her favor. After grabbing the wire cutters, she avoided her usual route in getting to the perimeter fence. She ducked between the tents in front of the area where the guards never patrolled. She slowly made her way to the rendezvous point and wanted to cry out in relief when she found Coop and Riley there waiting for her.

Holding the cutters out to Coop, she said, "Will these help?"

He sputtered his surprised thanks, then immediately started cutting an opening in the fence. While he worked, he said, "Memorize landmarks. It won't be as easy to remember the route under pressure in the dark, and we'll only have a short window to get Julia out safely. We'll wheel her on the gurney as far as we can, Angie, but you'll have to help me carry her after that."

Angie pulled the fence apart as Coop cut the links, but she stopped when she nicked her finger on a jagged edge of metal. "I'll do whatever you need. I'm tougher than I look," she said, as she shook her hand to ease the pain.

Riley stepped into her place and tugged on the unattached part of the fence. "You don't have to tell us. We've seen what you're capable of. This will be a cakewalk compared to surviving for a week in that crashed plane."

Coop finished cutting an opening big enough to allow them to get Julia through the fence. He stepped back to admire his handy work before pushing the fence back into place and handing the cutters to Riley. "Hide those in your pack. They'll come in handy later. A hundred things could go wrong on this little adventure. It might be smarter to stay."

Angie shook her head. "I know the risks, but I've got to get back to my family. I don't care what it takes."

"I'll wait for you in Julia's room in the infirmary until midnight. If you aren't there by then, I'm going alone. Riley, do your best to be here by one."

"I'll aim for that, but I can't guarantee what time I'll be back. You'll have to be patient. If I'm not here by four-thirty, get Julia back to the infirmary."

They all agreed and went through the plan once more to make sure they hadn't forgotten any details. With the plan cemented in her brain, Angie left first and made a note of the terrain as she headed to her tent. She made it back just before four, which gave her enough time to get almost three hours of sleep before she had to report for her shift.

"WAKE UP, SLEEPY HEAD," she heard Maisy saying as she shook her awake. "You'll be late for work."

Angie rolled over and stared up at her, trying to figure out what was happening. She was always the first one awake in the tent. Most of the time she was gone before the others stirred.

"What time is it?" she croaked.

"Almost seven. You okay? You're pale."

Angie gripped her stomach and moaned with pretended discomfort. "I was in the bathroom on and off all night," she said to cover her tracks in case any of them had heard her coming or going. "Must be something I ate."

Patricia studied her for a moment, then said, "It shows. You'd better report to your supervisor. She won't want you anywhere near the food in case what you have is contagious."

"Good idea."

She got up and slowly dressed before shuffling across the compound to the mess hall. She was relieved to see Paula, the one supervisor on duty who didn't treat her like dirt.

When she got a look at Angie, she said, "You look like hell. What's going on?"

Angie had to bite her cheek to keep from smiling. She felt perfectly fine, but everyone kept telling her how awful she looked. If it hadn't been working in her favor, she would have been offended.

"Stomach trouble. I had a rough night," she mumbled.

Paula pulled the top of her apron over her mouth and nose. "Get to the infirmary and don't come back to work until you're a hundred percent. We can't have you spreading disease around the food."

"Yes, ma'am," she said as she turned and bowed her head to hide her smile.

She had no intention of going to the infirmary, even though Riley or Coop would have vouched for her. She returned to her empty tent and had her best sleep since before the CME. It came at the perfect time since odds were, she wouldn't sleep that night. When she woke around four in the afternoon, she went to the kitchen to eat and load up on whatever food she could carry for their journey. The room was empty since it was the break between lunch and dinner meal services.

Back at her tent, Angie shoved the food she'd stolen into her pack along with a few other vital items. She left her other belongings in their usual places in the hope that no one would notice her missing pack in the morning. She, Coop, and Riley would need time to get as far away as possible before anyone noticed they were gone. With that finished, she spent an hour sneaking her pack into the woods near the fence. She camouflaged it with branches and leaves, then walked back to the camp without running into a single person. After a quick shower, she returned to her tent to wait for her roommates to come in before dinner.

"You look recovered," Maisy said when she came in and dropped onto her cot. "What did the docs say you have?"

Angie gave a backhanded wave. "Nothing but mild food poisoning. Not surprising around this place. All I needed was time and rest. I feel good as new."

"Good, you can join us for dinner," Anna said as she followed Patricia into the tent. "Glad it wasn't anything catching. Last thing we need these days is an epidemic of stomach flu."

"Not to worry. I'm fine," Angie said. "One of you will have to bring my plate to the fire pit. I'm not allowed in the mess hall until tomorrow."

"I'll get it," Patricia said. "Save us seats close to the fire."

Angie was so happy at having gotten away with her scheme that she didn't even think about her impending escape while she ate. She was chatty and friendly, which seemed to lift the spirits of the others. She'd felt a heavier than usual gloom hanging over the crowd when she first arrived at the fire pit but wrote it off to the dreary weather they'd had that day. By the time she left to go back to her tent, the mood had brightened somewhat.

After sleeping all day, she was wide awake at *Lights Out*, so she reviewed the escape plans step-by step in her head while her tent mates drifted off. Once Patricia was snoring, Angie pulled her boots on and slipped into her coat. When she was ready, she silently moved to the door but paused to say a final goodbye before going out into the frigid night.

"I'll do whatever is in my power to come back for you," she whispered. "Thanks, ladies for your friendship and kindness."

Tears blurred her vision as she walked to the infirmary. She wiped them away with her gloved fingers. It was no time to give into her emotions. She needed to be sharp for what was coming. When she was halfway across the compound and thought she was home free, some behind her yelled, "Halt."

She froze in her tracks and raised her arms in surrender, but she wasn't concerned. She was confident that it was one of the guards who would recognize her and let her go.

"Face me," the man ordered.

She slowly turned and was disappointed to realize it was a guard she'd never seen. He couldn't have been more than twenty, but he was tall and broad shouldered. Angie could see the bulge of his muscles through his coat sleeves.

He kept his rifle trained on her as he locked his eyes on hers. "Name?"

She had a false name on the tip of her tongue. She decided against that plan in case he took her in front of Branson or someone else who knew her real identity.

"Angie Hughes," she said calmly.

"What are you doing wandering around after curfew, Ms. Hughes?"

She swallowed the lump in her throat before saying, "Please, lower your weapon. I'm not armed."

He ignored her pleas and continued to glare at her. "I'm waiting for an answer."

As she scrambled for what to say, she considered telling him she was heading to the infirmary, but that would have led him straight to Coop and Julia. Instead, she decided on her usual excuse.

"I have terrible insomnia and go out walking every night. Ask the other guards. They never stop me and don't have a problem with it."

"I'm not the other guards, and I'll be reporting this behavior to Director Branson. No one is allowed out after curfew for any reason unless they're on duty of some sort." He stopped his lecture and squinted at her. "Are you acquainted with Dr. Poole? I thought I saw you with her at the fire pit yesterday morning."

"Yes, we're friends. Why?"

"She's missing. Know anything about that?"

Angie's gut tightened into a knot. "Missing? She said she and Brooks were going for a medical supply run. They're not back?"

He eyed her for a moment, then said, "That's none of your concern. Return to your quarters now."

Angie lowered her arms with a huff. "Fine but try not to shoot me in the back while I'm walking away."

He gave her a half-grin as he lowered his rifle. Her heart felt like it would pound out of her chest as she turned to go back to her tent. She'd left at 11:35 and guessed that it had to be close to 11:50. Coop had warned that if she wasn't in Julia's room by midnight, he'd leave without her. The only hope she had was that the guard would wander off far enough that she could sneak into the woods and meet Coop at the rendezvous spot. If the guard kept watch on her tent, she had no chance.

She dropped onto her cot and covered her face with her hands. They'd been deluding themselves to think they'd just walk out of the compound unscathed. And where were Riley and Brooks? They should have returned hours earlier. *We should have escaped yesterday with no dry run,* she thought as she peeked out the window flap to see where her watchdog was. He'd taken up position in the area just in front of their block of tents, blocking all chance of escape.

She quietly laid on top of her sleeping bag fully clothed so as not to disturb any of her roommates. She wanted to be ready to leave in a hurry if the guard left. If her tent-mates woke and saw her dressed, she'd say she'd been to the latrine. She folded her hands over her stomach and struggled to regain control of her thoughts. Riley had told Coop to wait until 4:30 before taking Julia back to the infirmary. That gave Angie four hours. The guards were bound to have a shift change before then. All she had to do was stay awake and wait. But now the guards seemed on the alert because of Riley's tardiness. The whole escape plan was unraveling.

To calm and distract herself, she fantasized about reuniting with her children and parents. She imagined finding someone to drive her home, then surprising the family by throwing the front door open and stepping inside with her arms open wide. They'd fall into her embrace, crying and laughing, beyond overjoyed to see her alive.

She ran through this pleasant, distracting scenario several times before Riley's words from the day before surged to the surface of her mind. The CME had struck the entire earth. Power was down across the globe, and billions could be dead within a year. *Will my family and I be counted among the dead?*

Another scenario rose in her innermost thoughts. What if she found her home in Allentown burned to the ground? Or worse, what if she opened the door only to discover the dead and frozen bodies of her children? The image sickened her. She nearly wretched up the food she had pounded down earlier in the day as her frightening thoughts were running wild.

Stop this, she ordered herself as she shook her head to clear it. The glowing dial on Anna's windup clock showed 2:30. Angie lifted the window flap to check on her guard. As she did, another guard she recognized from her nightly walks was coming toward him from the opposite side of the compound.

When he reached the new guard, he said, "What are you doing over here, Daniels? Your post is across the compound."

He glanced down and shuffled his feet. "I'm aware of that, sir. I caught Ms. Angie Hughes out after curfew for no reason. I escorted her back to her tent. I'm making sure she stays put."

"You're worried about Angie? She goes on her walkabout every night. Bad insomnia since her husband died in the plane crash. She's harmless. Your time would be better spent keeping an eye out for the insurrectionists than worrying about forty-year-old, unarmed women. You know Director Branson has been hearing murmurs of a possible uprising. You're relieved for now. Get some rest. You may be recalled for duty before the night is over."

Daniels gave a slight nod. "Yes, sir. Sorry, sir."

Angie stifled a laugh as the guard strode off with his head lowered and stuck her tongue out at his retreating back instead. His superior headed off in the direction of the perimeter fence where Angie was used to seeing him. She gave him five minutes to reach his position before hurrying out of the tent, hoping to find Coop and Riley waiting for her.

As she made her way through the woods to the rendezvous spot, she puzzled over what Daniels' superior had said about an uprising. She hadn't heard so much as a whisper about it. Not that she would since she had done her best to keep her distance from everyone. She hoped the rumors were true and that they'd be successful. It was about time someone took Branson and his minions out. She just hoped she wouldn't be around to see it.

She navigated her way through the trees and underbrush to reach the fence but came across patrolling guards at every exit point. She counted twice the number of sentries than were usually on duty at that time of night. It was the last thing she needed. After nearly thirty minutes of wandering, she found a clear spot. As she made a dash for the fence, she saw a black Humvee pass with the headlights off. In the glow of the dashboard lights, she could make out Coop behind the wheel. They were leaving without her.

She changed directions and took off at a full sprint to a shortcut that led to the main compound gate. She knew the perimeter road to the compound passed directly in front of the gate and the area was illuminated with mounted security lights. If she reached the gate before Coop, there was a chance he'd see her and do whatever it took to get her out.

She hadn't run so fast in decades. *Like my life depends on it,* she thought as she did her best to ignore the burning in her lungs and legs. She'd have plenty of time to recover once she was in the Humvee.

When she was a hundred yards from the gate, she was forced to leave the cover of the woods and tents to sprint into the open. Without checking for guards, she set her sights on the gate and ran with every ounce of strength she possessed. At twenty yards from the gate, she heard the Humvee before it came into view and her heart soared. Coop stopped and she could make out Riley watching her through binoculars. They'd seen her. She was going to make it!

Feeling a rush of adrenaline, she increased her speed, but at ten feet from the gate, Coop did the last thing she expected. He revved the engine and took off at top speed away from the compound. She and Riley locked eyes, and Angie read her anguish, but she was too late. Coop had made his choice. He was sacrificing her for the safety of Riley and Julia.

Angie hit the gate and tugged on the lock and chain as her one hope of freedom faded up the dark road. An instant later, two sets of hands were gripping her shoulders and arms. As the guards dragged her from the gate, she heard a woman's shrill scream. It took several moments for her to realize the screams were coming from her.

The guard on her right let go of her arm and clamped his hand over her mouth. "Shut it, lady. You'll wake the whole camp."

Angie stopped screaming but struggled to breathe through his fingers. When she was on the verge of passing out, she remembered her arm was free and pulled his hand off her mouth.

"Can't breathe," she said between gasps for air. "Won't scream."

The guard eyed her for a second, then put his hand back on her arm. She continued panting as they walked her to a part of the compound she'd never seen. It was near a bank of tents behind Branson's quarters. That had been the one area of the camp off limits to everyone except authorized personnel. The guard on Angie's left unlocked the gate to a smaller, internal fence that ran around the secured section, then shoved her inside.

Her anxiety mounted as she imagined all the terrible things they were going to do to her. "Where are you taking me?"

"To the lockup," a voice behind her that she recognized as her watchdog guard said. She turned to look at him over her shoulder. He had a sickening sneer on his face. "Knew you weren't as innocent as you pretended. Even had the boss fooled."

She felt tears threaten behind her eyes but refused to give in to them. She raised her chin, and said, "I don't know what you're talking about. I haven't done anything wrong. I couldn't sleep, so I went for a run. That's all."

"And just happened to end up at the main gate as your co-conspirators were escaping? Shows the kind of people they are, abandoning you to your fate. How do you feel about that?"

Angie's lip trembled as she said, "It was all a coincidence. I heard the truck and went to see what was happening."

He crossed his arms and glared at her. "And it just happened to be your best buddies stealing the Humvee to escape? We'll see what Director Branson has to say about your tall tale. Take her inside."

One of the guards gave her a shove to get her moving toward what looked like a wooden shed with a padlocked door. He unlocked and opened it, then stepped aside and motioned for her to enter. There was a single cot covered with a sleeping bag, a white paint bucket, a portable propane heater, and a metal washbowl resting on a small wooden cabinet.

From the doorway, he said, "Welcome to your new luxury accommodations. Hope you like it. You may be spending the rest of your life here unless you cooperate."

He gave her a half grin before closing and locking the door. Angie stood staring after him in stunned silence, her brain struggling to make sense of what had happened. Not ten minutes earlier, she'd been on the verge of escaping the vile compound. The next moment, she was a prisoner condemned to life in a seven-by-seven foot shed with one tiny window. She sank onto the cot, too numb to cry, too shocked to move. All she could think was how much she wished she'd perished on that plane with Grant.

CHAPTER 10

ANGIE HAD no way to gauge how long she sat frozen in place on her cot, but she estimated it had been close to nine hours. No one brought her food or even checked on her until the winter sunlight told her it was near one in the afternoon. She heard footsteps crunch on the frozen ground before the door flew open, and a female guard tramped in.

"On your feet," the woman ordered. "The Director wants to speak with you."

Angie had been expecting that and saw no reason to resist. It took three tries at standing before her numb legs would hold her weight. After her earlier cross-compound sprint followed by hours of immobility and freezing temperature, her muscles had grown numb and stiff. When she finally managed to remain upright, the guard took hold of her arm at the elbow and walked her to Branson's office. Two men shoveling snow off the gravel path stopped and stared when they passed. Angie ignored them. Hardly anyone in that compound meant anything to her.

Angie kept her eyes lowered when the guard told her to stand in front of Branson's ornate cherry wood desk. Out of the corner of her eye, she could see the man she knew as Warner leaning against a tent support in the corner. Everyone in camp knew Warner was Branson's hatchet man who carried out Branson's more disagreeable orders. His main job was to keep people in line. It was not a good thing to be the object of his attention. Angie shivered with fear when he stared at her without saying a word. She refused to look into his eyes.

She glanced up briefly to see Branson seated on the other side of the desk, watching her over the rim of his glasses. He was an ordinary looking man of average height and build, with thinning brown hair. He was probably in his forties. It was his dull, soulless brown eyes that made him so intimidating and creepy. Angie had done her best to keep her head down and avoid Branson since being taken hostage. He was a man of average intelligence, who was capable of committing atrocities without feeling remorse or regret in order to maintain power. That was how he'd maintained his grip of power in the compound. Well, that and the fact that he had somehow garnered the loyalty of toadies and psychopaths like Warner. She wondered again who he'd been before becoming Director Branson. *Probably some disgruntled bureaucrat,* she thought as he continued to study her.

"I've spent the past hour of my limited time trying to figure out what to do with you, Mrs. Hughes," he said, keeping his voice even. "Your level of cooperation and truthfulness to the questions I'm about to ask will determine that. Your fate is your hands. You've been a valuable member of this community since coming here. You've gone about your duties without causing trouble. You've worked hard and been an example to others. That is until your doctor friends arrived. I know you were in on their escape plot."

"Escape plot?" Angie said, mimicking her daughter Allyson's best innocent expression.

Branson leaned back and crossed his arms. "Nice try. My guards caught you at the gate trying to break out."

"Is that what they told you? That's not what happened. I was just out for a run when I heard a truck and went to see what was happening."

"Entertaining story. Let me tell you the kind of people your friends are. They stole a vehicle and supplies that didn't belong to them. They abandoned you with no thought of the consequences. They dragged their severely injured daughter out of her hospital bed into the freezing night. What kind of criminals would do that?"

It was almost comical for her to hear Branson calling Coop and Riley criminals. They were two of the best people she'd ever known. He was a depraved, tyrannical beast.

"Are you listening to me?" Branson asked, drawing her from her thoughts.

"Yes, sir," she mumbled.

"Good, because I haven't finished cataloging your friends' objectionable behavior. Dr. Poole drugged Commander Brooks, smashed him over the head with a blunt object, then left him to die. I had to waste precious resources to send someone out to rescue him. That's the kind of person you were willing to risk your comfortable existence safe from all the chaos and violence outside our gates."

As if on cue, Brooks strode in and handed Branson a paper with what looked like a handwritten list. He had a square of gauze taped to the crown of his head. Riley must have bandaged Brooks up after knocking him out. It was too professional to have been anyone else. She'd taken Brooks out to make her escape, but she'd had no intention of killing him. That much was clear. Angie would have given anything to hear that story.

As if reading her thoughts, Brooks turned and looked her in the eye for no more than a second. She'd expected to see anger or hostility, but his expression was void of emotion. His look confused her, but she wrote it off to his head injury. He left as quickly as he'd come without speaking a word.

Branson glanced at the list before laying it on the desk.

"Where are they going? What are their intentions? Do you have anything to say in your defense, Mrs. Hughes?"

Angie held his gaze for a moment, then gave a slight shake of her head. Nothing she said would change what happened next, and she refused to bow down to him. She had no doubt that he'd decided her fate before she set foot in his office. Branson signaled to the guard who took her arm and led Angie from the room. As they walked back to the shed, it occurred to Angie that her new home wasn't much different from her previous quarters. She almost preferred having a space to herself, and she'd be spared Patricia's snoring. It wasn't a bad tradeoff.

Before the guard closed the door on her way out, Angie said, "Am I allowed food? I haven't eaten since dinner last night."

The guard glanced at her but went out without answering. Angie wondered if the woman had been ordered not to speak to her to prevent her from poisoning her mind. Angie found that amusing until it occurred to her that Branson could be planning to starve her out. The Director would have a long wait if that were the case. Angie had become intimately acquainted with hunger and knew the limits of how far she could push herself. If Branson wanted a battle of wills, that was what she'd give him. She knew that everyone had a breaking point, but she would do her best to withstand Branson's pressure as long as possible.

ANGIE LAY on her cot trying not to count the passing minutes. Her jailers hadn't provided her with so much as a glow-stick for light. All she had besides the bucket, washbowl, heater, and cot were the clothes she'd worn when she was captured. The sun had set at least two hours earlier, but no one had come to her shed. She'd heard occasional muffled conversations beyond her walls, but nothing more.

"Starvation it is," she told herself as she rolled over onto her other side. For all her earlier brave thoughts of outlasting Branson, the truth was that her hunger pangs were growing stronger as she grew weaker. Like the other hostages, she'd lived on a diet that provided little more than basic calories and nutrients to sustain life. She wasn't exactly starting her starvation protest from a position of strength.

The other problem was water. She'd had nothing to drink since going to bed twenty-two hours earlier. People could survive for weeks with no food, but she'd only last three or four days without water at the most. Branson knew this and, if he wanted her dead, killing her through dehydration was a particularly vicious way to do it. Besides, it was an agonizing, terrible death. Angie had read about people stranded on life rafts with no water for days, who went insane before they died.

As images of her frail body drying up like a cornhusk in summer sun crept into her mind, she shook her head, then stood and began pacing. She'd have to find ways to keep her mind and body occupied to avoid letting her thoughts drift into darker places. It was possible she'd be a prisoner in that place for months if not years. She didn't blame Coop and Riley for leaving her, and she was thrilled they'd escaped, but that didn't make the reality of her situation any easier.

She was on her third lap around the tiny shed when she stopped in front of the cabinet and studied it for a moment, noticing for the first time that it had two drawers. She pulled the top one open and heard the contents shift as she did. She reached her hand inside and touched what felt like a flashlight. She picked it up and turned it in her hands until she found the on button. The glow was enough to illuminate the entire room. *You're such an idiot,* she thought as she pointed the beam into the drawer. Three water bottles lay on their sides along with a toothbrush, a bar of soap, a hand towel, a comb, and a roll of toilet paper.

She guzzled an entire bottle of water, then set the flashlight on its base on top of the cabinet as she opened the lower drawer.

Inside were a blanket, an extra pack of batteries, a legal pad, and a pen. She wrapped the blanket around her shoulders, then carried the pad of paper and pen to her cot along with the flashlight. She'd lost the journal she stared on the plane in the cottage fire, so she decided to start a new one. Writing out her thoughts would help her cope with the stress of her captivity and give her a constructive way to pass the time.

Not wanting to waste her flashlight's precious battery life, she'd keep her first journal entry short and decided to write subsequent ones during daylight hours. She chuckled as she started her first entry with how stupid she'd been not to check the cabinet drawers. She next wrote of her capture and all that happened since. She planned her entry for the following day to flash back to the day she and Grant left home for their trip. She hoped writing of all she'd survived and overcome would give her the strength to keep going.

She was putting the final touches on her entry when she heard the padlock on her door squeak just before the door swung open. Brooks came in carrying a covered tray and glass of what looked like orange juice. Angie's stomach growled loud enough for Brooks to hear as he placed the tray of delicious smelling food on the cabinet.

He turned to face her, then crossed his arms over his chest and studied her for a moment. When Angie began to grow uneasy under his scrutiny, he said, "Director Branson wants you to see that he's a patient and benevolent man. As a show of faith in his belief that you'll confess your crimes and return to the fold, he's allowing you benefits afforded to members of his loyal staff. Please understand his patience has limits, so don't delay your confession."

Angie gave him a slight smile before saying, "Thank Director Branson for me, but tell him I have no crimes to confess, and I won't bow to his will."

Brooks' emotions were guarded as he said, "I'll pass on your message to our gracious leader." Angie noticed that he'd raised his voice loud enough for whoever might be standing outside to hear. As he passed her on his way out, he leaned close to her ear and whispered, "Trust no one but me. Don't believe what they tell you. There are a few of us on your side in Branson's inner circle. We're doing what we can for you. Don't despair."

He straightened and hurried out before she could even acknowledge that she'd heard and understood him. Too hungry to make sense of his stunning statement, she grabbed the tray and carried it to her cot. She lifted the cover to reveal half a roasted chicken, mashed potatoes, green beans, and a slice of freshly baked bread. She was careful not to devour the luscious food, afraid her stomach wouldn't be able to handle all of it at once.

When she'd eaten as much as her shrunken stomach could comfortably hold, she pushed the tray aside and sat back to consider what Brooks had said to her. Her first and most obvious thought was that it was a trick. He hadn't asked for information or anything else from her, so until she knew more, she decided not to trust Brooks or anyone else.

The other possibility, that he was being honest, was almost too glorious to imagine. If true, the rumors of a possible coup would make sense. She still couldn't fathom any way that it could be possible. Those who opposed Branson were weak and didn't have access to weapons or any way to communicate plans to each other. Even if some of the conspirators were in Branson's inner circle, they were likely too few to overcome Branson's thugs. Angie recognized there was a lot she didn't know about the inner workings of Branson's circle of cronies. She was frankly bewildered by Brooks' statement and hoped beyond hope he was on the level.

They were matters too weighty for her to consider in her exhausted state, and they had nothing to do with her so far. What could she do from inside her little cell? She covered the tray and set it back on the cabinet for later. It was chilly enough in her shed that the food would stay fresh for her to eat when she was hungry again, even if she had to eat it cold. She brushed her teeth, then slid off her boots before climbing into her sleeping bag. Without the obligation of having to get up for her shift in the kitchen and nothing else to occupy her time, she could sleep as long as she wanted. As she closed her eyes with a sigh, she thought being a prisoner might not be such a terrible punishment after all.

AFTER A DEEP, dreamless sleep, Angie was startled awake when the guard from the day before yanked the door open, letting in the blinding morning sunlight. Angie covered her eyes as she sat up, then unzipped her sleeping bag and swung her feet to the floor and quickly put on her boots. With her eyes away from the doorway, she lowered her hand and watched the guard set another tray on her cabinet before picking up the one from her dinner. Angie closed her eyes and breathed in the delectable smell of pancakes and bacon. Apparently, Branson hadn't given up on her yet. If this was a tactic to get Angie to confess, it was a poor one. It would only make her stronger and more determined to resist. She would go along with it for as long as it lasted.

"What time is it?" she asked the guard on her way out. The woman turned and stared at Angie with a smile she couldn't decipher, then left without a word.

"Strange woman," Angie said as she jumped up to get her breakfast. She savored each bite as she cleaned the plate, even licking up the syrup. When she'd finished, she fell back on the cot and put her hands over her bulging stomach. She had no illusions that the royal treatment would last forever, but she was determined to make the best of it while it lasted. After resting for five minutes, she covered several pages of the notepad with a new journal entry until her fingers cramped. She then got up and ran through a series of exercises Maisy had taught her to stay fit.

All of that took about ninety minutes. Angie had no idea what she'd do to fill the empty time until lunch. She got back into the sleeping bag to try to nap, but she wasn't remotely tired after her full night's rest. She picked up the pad and pen and started a sketch of the shed. Though Angie had always been fascinated by art, she'd never been much of a sketch artist, but she did her best to recreate the view of the room. She worked until her hand grew tired, then put the pad aside and did fifty laps in the shed. Following that, she gave up trying to keep herself occupied and dropped back onto her cot. It was easy to understand how prisoners in isolation lost their minds from boredom.

Roughly an hour later, she heard the squeak of the padlock and wanted to jump for joy. That was until the door opened to reveal her watchdog guard from the night she tried to escape. He sneered at her as he set her tray down.

"I knew you'd end up in here. You might have had the other guys fooled, but I saw right through your innocent act."

"Yeah, you're a genius," Angie said with a huff. "This is all a misunderstanding, and I'll be free in a day or so."

His smile faded and his eyes narrowed as he stared at her. "Keep deluding yourself all you want. You have no idea what Branson has in store for you."

He turned on his heel and went out, slamming the door behind him. Brooks' words flashed in her mind. *Trust no one but me. Don't believe what they tell you.* She hoped with her whole being Brooks had told the truth.

She took her time with her lunch, stretching the meal out as long as she could. Her effort only used up twenty minutes. *What do I do for the next four hours?* she wondered as she shoved the empty tray aside. If Branson wanted to break her down, all he had to do was bore her to death. Maybe that was his plan.

She worked on her sketch for an hour before losing interest, then came up with the idea to write letters to her children and parents. The postal service no longer existed, but if she ever got free of the compound, she could hand deliver them. It would be proof for them that they had been in her thoughts from the moment she stepped on that fateful plane flight.

She was finishing the letter to Neal when she heard someone put a key in the door's padlock. *What now?* she thought as she got to her feet. When the door opened, a brisk wind blew in, and she caught a glimpse of drifts of snow piled three feet high. With no window, she hadn't known the weather had changed, but the snow explained why it had been so cold and quiet for the past twenty-four hours.

Warner sauntered in followed by Brooks and the watchdog, and she turned her attention to them.

Warner crossed his arms, and said, "We're here to give you one last chance to confess."

"What is it I'm supposed to be confessing to? Going for a run in the middle of the night? I'd done that several times since coming here. No one paid any attention to me. Or getting too close to the gate? I heard a truck and just wanted to see what was happening." She pointed at the watchdog. "Daniels told me Riley hadn't come back from her med run and I was worried. That's all that happened."

Brooks and Warner turned and glared at Daniels, but he just shrugged.

"So, you're determined to stick to that version of events?" Warner said. She nodded, then lowered her head, afraid he'd see the lie in her eyes. "Then, we're here to deliver Branson's sentence."

Angie took a step back. "Sentence? I haven't had a trial. This is still the United States of America, a country of which I'm a citizen who has rights. Who's Branson to be handing down sentences? Is he a judge? An elected official? He's nobody. Just some wannabe upstart taking advantage of innocent, vulnerable people."

Warner backhanded her across the mouth. The blow nearly knocked her off her feet. As she rubbed her throbbing cheek, she tried to catch Brooks' eye, but he avoided her gaze.

After a moment he said, "Rein it in, Warner. The Director didn't authorize you to discipline the prisoner. You know what a stickler he is for protocol."

Warner massaged the back of his hand, and sarcastically said, "Right. Lost my head. I apologize. Does that make you feel better Angie?"

Warner stepped closer to Angie, and she felt her panic rise. She should have known better than to mouth off to him. The walls started to close in on her with the four of them in the tiny shed. She took a few breaths which didn't help. She just wanted him to have his say and go.

Brooks glanced at her, then checked his watch. "Just get on with it."

"Mrs. Angeline Hughes, to make a public example of you and discourage others from following your actions, you are sentenced to execution by firing squad at the fire pit, noon tomorrow. Enjoy your final day on earth."

Warner shoved Daniels out of his way and moved toward the door. Angie's brain refused to accept what she'd just heard. Branson was going to murder her! Her throat muscles contracted, and she struggled to draw a breath. Warner and Daniels stepped out into the snow, but Brooks turned to face her and lifted his palm in a gesture of calm. She raised her eyes to his and felt his reassurance. Before she could speak, he was gone.

She sank to her knees on the cold floor, desperately trying to control her breathing. When her throat relaxed and the room stopped spinning, she crawled to the cot and climbed onto it. Brooks hadn't wanted the other two to see his gesture. What did it mean? Did he have the power to save her from a camp full of thugs? Her mind churned with questions, fear, and sadness. Fifteen minutes earlier, her biggest concern was boredom. Now, she was facing her own mortality.

She lay on her side, once again frozen in place as the snowstorm raged beyond her micro-prison. She'd finally reached her breaking point. After all she had gone through. She somehow had believed that she was not slated for death. She was the only survivor in a plane crash. God seemed to be preserving her life for some reason. She had been saved just to be murdered by these crazy men. It was inconceivable. Who was she that Branson needed to make an example of her? She was no one, and her indiscretion had been nothing. Certainly not worthy of death.

If Riley and Coop had known her fate, would they have acted differently? Would they have risked their safety for hers? Was it too late to tell Branson whatever he wanted to hear? Would he be willing to spare her? There were no good answers to her questions. All she could do was await her death. A seed of a thought crept into her head that maybe it was better to be out of the post-CME world than in it.

As she stared across the shed in the fading light, a rusty nail protruding from a broken board caught her eye. There was another way to deny Branson his satisfaction. She got off the cot and walked to the nail. All it would take was a hard stab into the side of her throat. She wasn't sure she was capable of such a thing. But trying to free the nail at least gave her a much-needed distraction. She put on the gloves her jailers had allowed her to keep and gripped the nail and tugged with all her might. It didn't budge. She shined the flashlight beam on it and saw the end was bent behind the board. Since the wood was cracked, she was sure she could still dislodge it.

She became so engrossed in getting that nail free, that she didn't hear the door open. It was only the gust of frigid air that broke her concentration. She spun around to see Brooks holding her dinner tray and staring at her with raised eyebrows. He put the tray down and reached her in three steps.

"What are you up to there?" When she just continued to stare at him, he pulled her hands away from the nail and studied it for a moment. "Now, none of that. Get back to your cot."

She obeyed without protest. Brooks took a folded multi-tool from his pocket and yanked the nail from the wall with a pair of pliers. After tossing it out into the snow and securing the door against the blasting wind, he stood staring down at her with his hands on his hips.

"I can guess what you were planning to do with that nail. I told you to trust me. That didn't look like trust."

Angie's shoulders slumped as she stared down at her gloved hands. "Give me a reason why I should trust you. I've been sentenced to death. Are you going to defy Branson and put a stop to my execution? You're one of his top minions." Brooks gave a quiet chuckle when she'd finished her rambling. "I don't see anything funny here."

"I just got an image of those movies when you said minion." He sank on to the cot beside her, and said, "Good lord, I miss movies. I miss texting my girlfriend and playing my fishing video game with my sons." He paused and stroked his chin. "I miss my sons. I hate not even knowing if they're alive."

Angie stared at him in shock. "You're a father?"

"Yes, of three strapping boys. Hard to believe, I know."

"Then how can you follow that monster?"

He leaned closer to her and lowered his voice. "I'll explain everything once this is over. I don't have much time. I'm only talking to you now because of the storm. Everyone is hunkered down. I can't prove to you that you can trust me. You'll just have to take a leap of faith. I give you my word that I'll sacrifice my life before I let anything happen to you. There is an uprising coming. We're just waiting for the right moment. This storm and your execution spectacle may have given us the perfect opportunity."

He got up and started to pace. "Just be ready for anything tomorrow. It may get rough, but you're used to that."

"I'll trust you. What do I have to lose at this point?" When his back was turned toward her, she saw the bandage on his head, and said, "What happened to your head? Did Riley do that to you?"

He raised his hand and pressed his fingertips to the bandage. "She has spirit that one. She drugged me, and I hit my head on the way down when my legs gave out. I'm sure she didn't mean for that to happen. She could have left me to die, but she stitched my wound and left me enough food and water to survive until help came. I didn't tell Branson that part. I had to make her out to be a villain."

Angie managed to laugh at that. "That sounds like our Riley."

"Thank her for me if you ever see her again."

"I never will. You'll have to do it yourself."

Brooks reached for her hands and helped her to her feet. "I have to go. Enjoy your dinner, and don't worry. I'll protect you, no matter what it takes. One vital thing to remember, when the time comes, hit the deck and don't move."

"And what time is that?"

"You'll know."

He let go of her hands and started to leave, but she caught hold of his wrist. "Why, Brooks? Why would you sacrifice yourself for me? You don't even know me."

"Simple. I was at the church. I was there when Julia was shot. I may not have committed those acts, but I stood by and did nothing to stop them. No matter how long I live, I'll never be able to make up for what I let happen. Saving you is just one small first step. Allow me that."

He pulled his coat close and hurried out before she could thank him. Maybe that was for the best. If things didn't go according to his plan, she might not have a reason to thank him.

ANGIE HAD HOPED for another restful night of sleep after Brooks' reassurances but had been disappointed on that front. She'd tossed and turned most of the night. When she finally fell asleep, she dreamed that Branson was preparing to behead her with a huge axe. That put an end to all hope of sleep.

She couldn't shake the feeling that Brooks and his cohorts were wildly optimistic they could overthrow Branson. Brooks hadn't shared the plan with her, so she could only trust they would succeed. She got up to use her bucket, brush her teeth, and comb her hair, not that it mattered. It was just comforting to follow her usual routine. With those tasks finished, she wrote out her final journal entry by flashlight beam. It no longer mattered if she used up the batteries.

Her uncommunicative guard showed up with the breakfast tray right on schedule an hour later. When she straggled in, Angie realized the storm had stopped but powdery snow coated the guard's pant legs up to her thighs.

As Angie watched the guard set her tray on the cabinet and uncover the food, she said, "How many feet did the storm dump?" She didn't expect a response, but it felt good to speak out loud.

With her back still to Angie, she said, "Has to be at least four feet. The boss has crews out working to clear the paths, but it's a big job. Director Branson sent a few guys out in the four-by-four trucks to see if they can round up some blowers."

Angie nearly fell off the cot in shock at hearing her speak. She sounded like a friendly person. Angie wondered why she hadn't spoken before until she realized it didn't matter anymore if she chatted with her prisoner. The woman expected Angie to be dead in a few hours, so what was the harm?

"Snowblowers would help," Angie said. "We had one at home. I'm from Allentown."

The guard turned to face her. "What are you doing here?"

Angie didn't feel like going into what had brought her to Virginia. "Long story," was all she was willing to say. "What's your name?"

She hesitated before answering. "Darcy. Darcy Meade."

"Thanks for braving the drifts to bring my breakfast, Darcy."

She gave Angie a smile that didn't reach her eyes. "Least I could do."

"I think my heater's about out of fuel. Think you could get someone to bring a replacement tank."

"I'll see what I can do," Darcy said, laughing as she went out.

"Guess I won't be seeing that propane," Angie whispered as Darcy closed and locked the door.

She wasn't as enthusiastic about her meal that morning but polished all of it off. If all hell broke loose like Brooks predicted, it could be a while before she had another hot meal. When she'd finished, she slammed her dishes and the tray against the wall as a show of defiance, like people always did in movies. It was not as satisfying as she'd expected. The sight of the mess scattered on the floor actually made her laugh. The act might have had a more profound effect if the dishes had been ceramic instead of metal.

The heater sputtered out seconds later and the temperature plummeted in minutes. She crawled into her sleeping bag and pulled the blanket over top. If no one brought propane, Branson's executioner could find her dead of hypothermia. She tried to sketch but her hands got too cold whenever they slipped out from under the sleeping bag. She considered getting up to do jumping jacks to get warm but couldn't bring herself to leave her cocoon. Her only recourse was to stay covered and wait for doom to arrive.

After her lack of sleep during the night, she drifted off at some point and was awakened to the sound of the door opening.

"Geez, it's freezing in here," a male voice she didn't recognize said. "Think she's still alive?"

"Who's the moron who let the heater go out?" Brooks asked. "If she's dead, whoever's responsible will be next."

Angie threw the sleeping bag off and sat up. "I'm not dead yet," she said. "I asked Darcy for a replacement tank, but no one brought it."

"I'll pass that on to the Director," Brooks said. "On your feet. It's almost noon."

Angie grunted as she swung her feet to the frozen floor. After pulling on her boots and lacing them, she got to her feet and said, "You're really going through with this? You're actually going to murder me in front of everyone?"

"With pleasure," the guard standing beside Brooks said.

Brooks elbowed him to quiet him and trained his eyes on Angie. "Having second thoughts?"

"Yes. I'll confess to whatever Branson wants me to say. Take me to him."

"You should have spoken up sooner. It's too late now. The boss is in a mood and hungry for blood. Yours is as good as any."

"You're disgusting, Fletcher," Brooks said. "This is a legal proceeding not a vampire flick. He's right, though, Mrs. Hughes. I'm sorry, but it is too late. Let's go."

Angie backed up and pressed her body against the back wall. "How can you do this? Branson's insane. You don't have to obey him."

Her reaction was partly an act and partly instinctive. What if Brooks' story is a complete fabrication just to keep me from making a scene at the execution. If so, it must be the cruelest trick ever played on a human. If he had been honest, what if his people couldn't save her? What if the plan failed because Branson knew about the planned coup? If one aspect of their plan misfired, she'd be dead. Brooks gave an exasperated sigh and signaled toward her with his head. Fletcher lunged for her and yanked her away from the wall, then cuffed her wrists.

When Fletcher reached for her elbow, Brooks said, "I'll take her from here. Go alert the boss that we're on our way."

Fletcher nodded and took off at a trot. When he was out of earshot, Brooks wrapped his gloved fingers around her arm, and whispered, "Convincing performance. Keep it up."

"It wasn't all an act," she said quietly as she let him lead her from the shed out onto the snow packed path. "I'm really scared."

"Don't be. Everything's in place. You won't be harmed."

"How can you be so confident? You saw how excited Fletcher is to see me dead."

Brooks leaned his head close to hers. "Branson is skilled at what he does. He's brainwashed these morons to believe you, Coop, and Riley are dangerous threats to the community. If the captives find out how easy it was for Coop and Riley to escape, others might follow, and Branson's house of cards comes crashing down. His goons know what that means for them if it does, and that's exactly what we're going to make happen today. I can't say more now. Trust us."

Angie nodded, and whispered, "Doing my best. Really, I have no choice. My options are kind of limited."

"That's the spirit," Brooks said in a quiet voice. He straightened up and tightened his grip on her arm. She knew it was for show, but it did nothing to calm her. When they reached the central square, Angie was astounded to see the entire area around the fire pit had been cleared of snow. Branson must have had his hostages and thugs working since dawn. A fire blazed in the pit, and Angie welcomed the warmth.

Brooks positioned her six feet from the pit, then released her arm. Angie scanned the surrounding area and was surprised to see more than a hundred pairs of curious eyes trained on her. She recognized a few, including Dashay, the nurse who'd been at Julia's bedside in the infirmary. Her former tent-mates weren't visible until Maisy broke through the front of the crowd and rushed toward her.

"It's Angie!" she cried. "We thought you were dead."

Two women who were undoubtedly part of the Branson team grabbed Maisy's arms and yanked her back into the crowd. As Angie watched the scene, she wondered why Maisy had assumed she was dead.

What does it matter? Angie thought as she continued to scan the crowd. Her heart sank at the sight of Branson's other guards holding weapons and stationed in equal positions around the outside of the crowd. How did Brooks' people have any chance of overpowering them?

She heard a commotion behind her and turned to see the crowd part as Branson strode through the break, followed by Warner. They stepped to either side of Angie, and she was afraid she was going to be sick.

Branson raised his hands to quiet the crowd, then said, "I'm sure you're wondering why we've gathered you here."

They don't know, Angie thought. *He hasn't told them he's planning to murder me in front of their eyes.*

"I had a long and impressive speech planned, but apparently Mother Nature has other ideas. So, I'll keep it brief so we can all get back inside. This woman beside me is Angie Hughes. She was captured trying to escape from camp after conspiring with Drs. Cooper and Poole. We've given her multiple opportunities to confess her crimes and give up her co-conspirators' location, but she has refused even though she was caught in the very act of escape. As a result, after deep deliberation, we've been forced to sentence her to death by firing squad."

Murmurs and shouts of protest arose from the crowd.

A tall, broad shouldered man Angie didn't recognize pushed his way into the open and locked his eyes on Branson. "Did you just say you're going to execute this woman?"

As Warner shoved Angie to her knees, Branson casually answered, "Yes."

In a flash, the man smashed his fist into Branson's face. The murmurs became a roar and she heard Brooks shout, "Now." The crowd erupted and hostages took off running in all directions toward the guards. When the first shots rang out, Angie dropped flat to her stomach, hitting the deck just as Brooks instructed. Her hands were still handcuffed behind her, leaving her vulnerable. There was nothing else she could do but wait. She squeezed her eyes shut and expected to be struck by a stray bullet.

The chaos continued for two or three minutes, but to Angie it felt like an eternity filled with gunshots, people shouting curses, and men and women fighting. When the roar began to fade, she opened one eye in time to see an unarmed Warner crumple to the ground.

Angie turned her head away when she saw blood spreading in the snow around him. She opened both eyes and was relieved to see Brooks chasing Branson towards the edge of the clearing. Brooks overtook him in seconds and tackled him into the snow, then put him in a choke hold and jerked him down to his knees. Sunlight flashed off the blade as Brooks raised a knife and drew it across Branson's throat. When Branson went limp, Brooks released his body and climbed to his feet. He turned to where Angie still lay on the frozen ground and held her gaze for a moment before bending over and vomiting into the snow.

"The boss is dead," someone shouted. "Let's get out while we can."

Angie saw at least five guards take off toward the main gate. Then the melee ended as abruptly as it began, and the world grew quiet except for the occasional cry for help. Brooks, Maisy, and Patricia rushed to Angie's side and helped her to her feet. Brooks pulled out the key to unlock her cuffs. Angie rubbed her wrists as she stared at Brooks in awe.

"You did it," she whispered. "That was the most heroic act I've ever seen."

"I owed it to you," Brooks said. "It was my fault you were here in the first place."

Brooks flinched when Maisy ran up to him and threw her arms around him. "I thought you were a bad guy, but you're really a hero, which is a rare thing these days." Tears formed in her eyes. "We're free! You saved us."

Brooks put his hands on his hips and lowered his head. "It's true we're free but please don't ever call me a hero."

Maisy grinned at him. "If that's what you want, but you can't stop me thinking it."

Brooks nodded. "Fair enough."

The four of them grew quiet as they looked over the aftermath of the coup. Angie counted seven hostages' bodies and ten dead guards. She was sickened by the pointless loss of life but was also surprised the death toll wasn't higher. The rest of the former hostages spotted them standing near the fire pit and started gathering around. A few were dragging Branson's minions who hadn't managed to escape.

"What happens now, Boss?" Maisy asked Brooks as they all looked to him.

"Don't call me that either. Why would I be the one in charge?"

Dashay, who was standing near the front, said, "You were third in command after Warner. You know how the camp runs better than anyone else."

The Army medic named Nico Mendez, who ran the infirmary before Riley and Coop, was standing next to Dashay. He stepped forward, and said, "Dashay's right. Someone needs to be in charge until we get organized. It should be you."

Nods and murmurs of agreement rippled through the group.

"Fine," Brooks said. "I'll take temporary charge until we can elect a mayor and ruling council." Applause broke out, but Brooks waved his arms to silence it. "I'm honored to get this community operating the way it should have been from the beginning. I offer my sincerest apologies for the pain or trouble I caused any of you. I learned early on that Branson was a psychopath and began plans to overthrow him. I'm sorry it didn't happen sooner. When Branson told me he was going to execute Angie, I knew his time was up."

"Apology accepted," Marcus said. "We'll do whatever you need us to."

Brooks gave him a quick nod. "I'm grateful. First off, anyone who'd like to leave is free to go. We'll arrange to send you off with whatever supplies we can spare. All I ask is that you give us a few days to get organized first. You won't get far in this snow anyway."

As Angie listened, she couldn't hold back her emotions. She had escaped death again due to Brooks' heroic actions. She'd be on her way to see her children in a matter of days. Her joy was more than she could bear.

"Our next order of business is to deal with the deceased. Mendez, you can take care of that. Gather whatever help you need. Finally, we need to deal with Branson's remaining loyal followers. Until we can figure out what to do with them, we'll have to keep them locked up for the safety of the rest of the camp. Weaver, are you here?"

The broad-shouldered man who'd punched Branson made his way up to Brooks, and said, "Here, Boss."

"Get our guys and hold Branson's people in the supply tent. I'll be with you as soon as I can."

Weaver gave a loud whistle and gestured for his people to follow him. The crowd cheered as his men led Branson's stragglers toward the camp headquarters. Most of them were already renouncing their fallen leader. Many of them would have to be tried for their crimes.

Brooks turned back to face the crowd. "I know you're cold, hungry, and probably overwhelmed by this turn of events. Honestly, I am too. To alleviate some of that, I'd like anyone on the kitchen staff to report to the mess tent and prepare lunch, only this time, make sure everyone is served equal and generous portions. The rest of you, please return to your usual duties for the time being. We'll make more suitable assignments as soon as we can assess our needs and capabilities."

As the crowd broke up to begin life under a new regime, Angie pulled Brooks into a tight hug. When they stepped apart, she said, "I'm proud of you. You were made for this leadership role."

"Hardly," he said with a laugh. "No one who knew me before the CME would have agreed with you."

"Then you weren't living up to your potential."

"That I will agree with, but how many of us do?"

"An excellent question to ponder another time."

"But Angie, this changes very little. Our world has been transformed irrevocably. Nothing has changed outside the wire. So, let's keep this in perspective."

Thanks for pouring cold water on a beautiful moment. But you aren't wrong, my friend. I'll worry about one that tomorrow.

"Fair enough!"

As Angie started to move away to go to the mess hall, Brooks reached for her hand to stop her. "Where are you going?"

"To help in the kitchen. That was my job before the recent insanity."

"I have a much more important role than serving in the kitchen. I'd like you to be my chief advisor. The job comes with Branson's personal quarters. Interested?"

Angie shivered. "I don't think I could stay in the place where that monster lay his head." She kicked at a pile of snow before looking him in the eye. "Thanks for the offer and your faith in me, but I'm not staying, Brooks. If I hadn't been caught trying to escape, I may have made it home by now. When the snow melts and it gets a little warmer, I'm taking off."

"I figured you'd say that, but I had to ask. In that case, I'll send you off with a vehicle of your choosing and enough fuel to get you home. It's freezing out here. Come with me to Branson's office."

Once they were inside, Angie pointed at the desk. "That's yours now. Take a seat."

He glanced at the desk, then shook his head. "First thing I'm going to do is destroy that monstrosity. It'll make great firewood. A piece of plywood propped on logs is all I need for a desk." He folded his arms and walked to the window. "In fact, I'm going to clear out all Branson's junk. Evil vibes."

"I don't blame you." She joined him in staring out the window, and said, "I couldn't have done what you did. How are you holding up?"

Brooks rubbed his face before answering. "It's too soon to say. I think I may be a little in shock. If someone had told me before the CME that I was capable of slitting someone's throat, I'd have thought they'd lost their mind."

Angie put her hand on his shoulder. "Your reaction is natural, but this isn't the same world that existed a month ago. You had no choice but to take Branson out. Many more innocent people would have died if not for you. Think of what happened as a battle in wartime because that's what it was. No one will ever hold it against you."

He turned to face her, and his struggle was evident in his eyes. "I understand all of that logically, but the reality of what I did sickens me. I'm not sure I'll ever get over it."

"That's why we call people who do what you did heroes. No one steps into that role willingly."

"I'll never see myself that way, but I appreciate you saying that. It helps." He wiped his eyes, and said, "Enough of this. Let's go enjoy our victory feast."

Angie squeezed his hand, then followed him out into the cold. "Wouldn't miss it."

Chapter 11

"All set?" Patricia asked as Angie tossed her pack into the Humvee seven days after the coup.

"Couldn't be more ready," Angie said as she hugged her. "You didn't have to come see me off. We said our goodbyes last night."

"Yes, we did," Maisy said after giving her a final hug. "Part of me wishes I was going with you."

"Grab your stuff," Angie said. "We'll squeeze you in somewhere."

Maisy took hold of Patricia's hand. "Thanks, but I belong here. Patricia's like a mom to me now, and Brooks says he needs someone with my energy and enthusiasm. You have your family waiting for you. Good luck, Angie. We'll miss you, even more now we lost Anna."

"I still can't believe she's gone," Angie said. "Such a senseless loss of life." The other two women nodded as they remembered their tent-mate who'd been mortally wounded on the day of the coup. "You'll have to honor Anna's memory by making Victoryville the wonderful community you all deserve."

Patricia blew Angie a kiss as she climbed into the Humvee. "Travel safe."

Angie nodded and pulled the door closed. "I'm ready," she told the other five occupants. "Thanks for waiting."

"We understand," the young woman named Jessica seated next to her said. "As horrible as it was at times, this place became like home. Can't say I'm sorry to be going though."

Angie nodded, then turned her thoughts to events of the past week as the driver, Spence, put the vehicle into gear. Brooks had done a masterful job of reorganizing the camp but had refused to run for mayor. He agreed to serve on the council. He planned to leave on a new adventure once the snows melted in the spring. A nurse with a beautiful Irish accent named Claire became the mayor. The group elected five others besides Brooks to serve on the council. Their first action as the new governing body was to hold a vote for the name of their community. Victoryville was the overwhelming winner.

Before the election, Brooks gave Branson's followers the choice to surrender and become contributing members of the community or leave. Half chose to strike out on their own. Others were exiled from the community because of their crimes under the Branson reign. No one was sad to see them go. Most of the ones who remained had joined Branson out of self-preservation and had not committed any major abuses. They had no trouble integrating with the rest of the residents. Angie wondered about the few others who were more reluctant to acclimate. There were always people who rocked the boat. She hoped they wouldn't cause trouble for Brooks down the line.

She leaned back and closed her eyes as Spence maneuvered the Humvee onto the highway. About half of the snow had melted but the two feet that remained still posed a challenge. Brooks had tried to persuade Angie's group to postpone for another week like the other thirty percent who'd chosen to leave, but they were anxious to move on. Their journey might take longer, but they'd be heading in the right direction.

Angie had made a point to get to know her fellow travelers in the three days since Brooks had organized their group. Spence and his wife, Alicia, were heading home to Hartford, Connecticut. They'd become stranded in northern Virginia on their way home after spending the holidays with their daughter's family. The CME had fried their car's computer, so they were on foot, looking for a place to go when one of Branson's men picked them up.

Jessica had been a student at Georgetown in DC when the CME struck. She and four friends decided to leave the city when things spiraled out of control four days after the CME strike. Jessica was the only one who survived. She was going home to her parents in Philly where she'd grown up. Spence and Alicia had offered to take her with them if her parents were gone.

Angie hadn't met the last two passengers, Benjamin and Anthony, until that morning. As they rode along, they explained that they'd traveled to Virginia on business from Brooklyn, New York. They'd been waiting to catch their flight home when the airport closed before the CME struck. Benjamin had wanted to wait in the airport until the power came back on, but Anthony was his supervisor and had insisted they take one of the few working cars they found in the rental lot to drive home. They'd been shielded in the airport from the horrors taking place outside but got a rude awakening once they were on the road. They were carjacked on the second day. Brooks found them stranded on the side of the road and took them to the compound.

"If I had listened to Ben, we'd have been safe in the airport all this time," Anthony told them. "He'd be in his rights to never forgive me for the things we've been through."

"You can't know that," Angie said. "Food and water would have run out by now if the travelers stranded at the airport remain there, and how would you have stayed warm?"

"Exactly what I keep telling Anthony," Benjamin said.

"I'm surprised the backup generators failed," Spence said.

"You'd think the ones in an airport like Dulles would have been hardened."

Benjamin nodded. "That's what we've wondered. The generators might have just needed to be turned on and no one at the airport knew how to do that. There were rumors that power was still on in the control tower, but it was dark when we left."

Anthony waved off his comment. "That's all moot now. All that matters is finding out if my wife and kids are alive and safe."

"Same for me," Angie said. "I left my son and daughter with my parents. I'm hoping for the best, but who knows."

After the others nodded or murmured in agreement, they all grew quiet. As they rode along, Angie considered the various reasons they'd ended up in Virginia and remembered Coop and Riley. Coop hailed from Chicago and Riley from Colorado. How many thousands or even millions had been stranded far from home? It would be delusional to expect to find life unchanged whatever their destinations might be. All they could do was hope and pray for the best.

THEIR FOUR-DAY JOURNEY to Philadelphia was slow and cold but uneventful. The world had been quiet, buried under its blanket of snow. They were fortunate that the weather held until they reached Jessica's parents' house when the first flakes began to fall. Even though the Humvee was a gas-guzzler, they were able to find plenty of cars to siphon off gas for the journey. They breathed a collective sigh of relief to find their modest, well cared for home in a middle-class suburb intact.

As soon as Benjamin shifted into park, Jessica flew from the truck and trudged through the knee-high snow to the front door. After twisting the knob and finding the door was locked, she pounded with her gloved hand with all her might. Angie couldn't hold back her tears when the door swung open thirty seconds later and Jessica's parents stood on the stoop, staring at her with their mouths hanging open. When they'd recovered from their shock, they'd pulled Jessica into their arms and held her like they'd never let go. Two men stepped behind her parents waiting for their turn to hug her. Jessica's travel companions took what they were witnessing as a good omen while they unloaded Jessica's belongings.

Jessica's parents insisted on feeding everyone lunch before sending them back out into the cold. While they all feasted on hearty chicken noodle soup, fresh baked bread, and peach cobbler, Jessica's parents recounted their experiences since the CME. Her father told of how after researching CMEs on the internet, he'd run to the local home repair warehouse and had bought the last three portable solar generators. The salesman talked him into purchasing Faraday bags to protect them from the CME. Her father then rented a truck to carry his treasures home and gave the installer a cash *incentive* to help him set up the generators that afternoon. Jessica's mother had told him he was overreacting, but she was grateful for once that he'd ignored her. The CME hit that night. They would have been without power if he hadn't acted so quickly.

Other than their constant worry over Jessica, their lives had been quiet, even boring at times. The biggest challenge had been securing food, but they'd managed better than most. Jessica's two brothers and their families had lived within an hour's drive but had made their way to Philly after the CME. They'd stayed when they saw how well their parents were surviving. All that was missing was Jessica.

"You've been unbelievably fortunate. Your situation is worlds better than what we've seen," Spence said. "We're glad you've been shielded from the horror out there."

Jessica's parents and brothers glanced at each other before her father said, "Not completely shielded. We've lost neighbors, friends." He paused for a moment and caught Jessica's eye. "And my parents."

Jessica slowly rose to her feet. "Gma and Gpa? They're dead?"

Her father stared at his hands resting on the table and nodded. "Yes. I'm sorry, Jess. We couldn't get our hands on the medications they needed. We were with them when they died."

Jessica's eyes glistened with tears as she wrapped her arms around her father's shoulders. "I guess it was too much to expect that the entire family would survive unscathed. I'm grateful I got to spend the holidays with them. I couldn't have imagined it would be for the last time."

When Jessica returned to her seat, her mother said, "Tell us what your experiences have been."

Angie stood before anyone had time to speak. "We'll leave it to Jessica to fill you in. We need to make it to my home in Allentown before dark, and the snow is picking up."

The four traveling on with her got to their feet and started putting on their coats.

"We can't thank you enough for the wonderful meal. We haven't had hot food for days," Anthony said.

Jessica's father stood and shook his hand. "It's a small price to pay for returning our girl to us. We wish you all the best in your journeys home."

AFTER SAYING their heartfelt goodbyes to Jessica, the five of them headed back out into the cold. The drive from Philly to Allentown usually took ninety minutes, but Angie knew with the weather and having to dodge debris hidden beneath the snow it would take two to three times longer than that. Since she knew the roads they'd travel, she took her place behind the wheel. She was glad to have the distraction of concentrating on driving since she was nervous at what she'd find at home.

When they'd been driving for five minutes, Alicia said, "What do you think the odds are that the rest of us will find our homes and families in such good condition as Jessica's?"

"I'd say five to ten percent," Anthony said.

"If that," Spence added. "They're living in a bubble. None of us should expect similar situations."

"I've always considered myself a positive person, but I have to agree with Spence," Benjamin said. "We should be preparing for the worst."

Angie exchanged a look with him through the rearview mirror. "That sounds rational in theory, but I can't even bring myself to imagine the worst. I buried my own husband in a snow drift. I'm not sure I'd survive much worse."

"You might be forced to," Anthony said. "If I've learned nothing else during my time under Branson's rule, it's that I can handle much more than I thought I could."

"We all have," Spence said. "Enough of this doom and gloom. We're free of the camp. We're all headed home. Let's focus on that."

"I'm all for that," Alicia said. "How much longer, Angie? The roads don't seem too bad here."

Angie glanced at the dashboard clock. "I'd estimate two and a half hours. If we can maintain this pace, we should make it by sunset. I hope you'll stay the night. I wouldn't want to send you out to travel in the dark."

"You won't have to twist my arm," Anthony said.

They went on to talk of their friends and families and what their lives were like before the world turned upside down. Angie was relieved they'd changed the subject. She was trying not to imagine what she'd find at home. It would be what it was.

When they were twenty miles outside Allentown, the highway

suddenly became clear of snow and debris. They crested a hill to find plow trucks lined up in an empty shopping center parking lot below. Houses with lights dotted the landscape reaching out for miles. The majority were dark, but it was an encouraging sight. Angie began to hope that Allentown hadn't been hit as hard by the effects of the CME as northern Virginia had.

They covered the distance into town in half the time they'd expected, but Angie was disheartened to see the neighborhoods leading up to hers in complete darkness and devoid of signs of life. When they were a few blocks from her house, she stopped the truck and shifted into park. Her hands trembled on the steering wheel as she stared into the blackness before her.

"I can't keep going," she mumbled. "This was such a vibrant community. It looks like a ghost town."

Alicia squeezed Angie's shoulder. "You've come too far to quit now. What if your children have given up, thinking you're dead? What if they're at home waiting for their mom to walk through the door? But if the worst has happened, we're here to help you through it."

Angie put her hand over Alicia's. "That's what I needed to hear. Thank you. And you're right. I have no choice but to face whatever I find."

She straightened her shoulders and shifted into drive. If the unthinkable had happened, if she'd lost her children and parents, she still had a sister and her family living twenty miles away. If they were gone too, she had her new family inside that truck.

She turned the last corner onto her block and pulled to a stop in front of her house. It was completely dark, but still standing unlike the many of hundreds of houses they'd passed on their journey. When she unbuckled her seatbelt, Spence and Alicia unbuckled theirs too.

Spence climbed out and opened the door for her. "We're going with you. You're not going to face this alone."

Angie nodded as she got out of the Humvee. Spence and Alicia moved to either side of her and took her hands as they approached the door. Angie's hand shook when she reached for the handle. She took a breath and turned the knob slowly. The door was unlocked and easily swung open. Angie's heart pounded so violently as she clicked on her flashlight and stepped inside that she feared it would explode in her chest.

Spence and Alicia turned on their flashlights, too, and followed Angie inside. As they shined the beams around the living room, it was obvious no one had been in the house for weeks at least. Dust coated the floor and every surface, and the room was nearly as cold as the outside.

"We'll check the whole house, but they're not here," Angie whispered. "What can it mean?"

Alicia, who had moved into the kitchen, called out for them to join her. When Angie walked in, Alicia handed her a piece of notepaper. Angie moved it close enough to read and shined the flashlight on it.

Dear Mom,

You can't even know how much I hope you'll find this letter. Nana and Grandpa died, but Neal and I are safe. Uncle Joel and Aunt Lanie came to take us to their house. Come as soon as you see this.

Love, Allyson

The letter was dated two weeks earlier. Angie gasped for air as her emotions threatened to tear her in two. Her parents were dead, but her children were alive. At least they'd been alive when Allyson wrote the letter. When the room began to spin, and Angie felt the strength draining from her legs, Spence put his arm around her waist and helped her to a chair at the table.

"What is it?" Alicia asked as she took the chair beside her.

Angie handed her the note, then rested her elbows on the table and sobbed into her hands. When Alicia finished reading, she handed the paper to Spence. He dropped into the chair beside his wife, and they quietly waited for Angie to have her cry. Anthony and Benjamin came in two minutes later. Spence walked them to the front room. When Angie was finally able to quiet her sobs, she wiped her face on her sleeve and got to her feet. She hurried into the living room with Alicia on her heels.

"I have to go to them," she said in a rush. "If you don't want to go with me, I'll find another way. Maybe one of our cars will still run."

Anthony took hold of her hands. "We didn't come this far to abandon you now. How far is it to your brother's house?"

Angie shook her head. "Brother-in-law and sister. Twenty miles. They live just outside of town on five acres. They have horses, and I think they have a generator."

"Doesn't matter," Alicia said, as she led Angie toward the stairs. "Do you want to pack some of your things? You may not be back here for a while."

Angie nodded and grabbed the stair rail. "Right. Good idea," she said as she started climbing. "Scavenge through the house. Take whatever you think we might need."

Fifteen minutes later, they were back on the road. The storm had accelerated to near blizzard conditions, but Angie was determined to keep going. She handed the wheel over to Spence who had the most experience driving in poor weather conditions. They'd siphoned the gas out of Angie and Grant's cars into the gas cans Brooks gave them, so if they got stopped on the road, they'd have enough fuel to keep the Humvee running through the night.

It took almost two hours to travel the twenty miles, but Angie wanted to shout for joy when she saw the lights burning inside her family's house. Her children were waiting for her behind those walls.

Angie told Spence to drive over to the snow-covered lawn and pull up as close to the house as he could get. When he braked to a stop, Angie sprang from the car and raced up the icy steps as quickly as her legs would carry her. She tried the knob but wasn't surprised to find the door locked. She pushed the doorbell button and was delighted to hear it ringing over the roar of the wind.

It was 8:15 pm in the middle of a blizzard, so she wasn't surprised that it took nearly two minutes for someone to answer the door. The curtain over the window next to the door moved aside. Neal peered out, then threw the door open and lunged at her. They toppled over, laughing and crying as they rolled in the snow hugging each other.

Allyson appeared in the doorway seconds later wearing a bathrobe and a towel wound around her hair. "What in the world are you doing, Neal?" she said with her hands on her hips.

Neal let go of Angie and scrambled to his feet. Pointing to Angie still lying in the snow, he said, "Look, it's Mom!"

Allyson bent over and squinted at Angie, then reached for her hands and pulled her to her feet. They stared at each other for an instant before Allyson threw her arms around her mother. They cried on each other's shoulders as Neal clung to the two of them. Angie felt the same elation as she had when her children were born. It felt so right to hold them in her arms that she wasn't sure she'd be able to let go.

When Angie heard footsteps in the hall, she glanced up to see her sister racing toward the doorway. When their eyes met, Lanie sank to her knees and stared at her in stunned silence. Allyson and Neal released their mom and moved out of the way. Angie knelt in front of her sister and wrapped her in her arms.

"Is it you, Angie? Are you really here?"

Angie pulled away and laughed through her tears. "I'm here. It's been a long, unbelievable journey, but I made it home."

As they got to their feet, Neal said, "Mom, where's Dad?"

Angie steeled herself to deliver the bad news. As joyous as their reunion had been, this was the moment she'd dreaded. She put an arm around each of her children, and said, "Your father was killed when our plane crashed on the day of the CME. I'll tell you the whole story later, but for now, I want you to know that his last thoughts were of you. He loved you more than anything in this world."

Allyson laid her head on Angie's shoulder, and said, "I knew, Mom. I can't explain it. I always knew you were alive. But something told me Dad didn't make it."

"It's true," Neal said through his tears. "When we were alone after Nana died, Ally told me Dad was dead. I didn't believe her. How could she know? But she was right."

"She told us, too," Lanie said. "I'm so sorry. That sounds lame, I know, and doesn't make it any easier. Grant was the best of men."

"That's not lame, and I appreciate it. It's been rough, but I've had some time to get used to the idea of life without him. I've been through so much since the crash that I've hardly had time to think about him."

"There will be time to tell us when you're ready." Lanie squeezed her hand and smiled. "I can hardly believe you're here."

"Lanie, where's Joel?" Angie asked, afraid to hear the answer.

"He's showering," she said with a laugh, then put her hands to her mouth. "He doesn't know. I have to tell him."

As she started off, Angie said, "Wait, I have some people with me. They can't go out into that storm tonight. Do you mind if they stay?"

"Of course, they can. You didn't need to ask. Get them in here."

Allyson looked down at her robe. "I'd better get dressed if I'm going to meet people. Neal, put your boots and coat on and help Mom bring the stuff in."

Angie smiled as she watched her daughter go. Something about her was different. She seemed older, more mature. It wasn't surprising after what she and Neal had been through. It was enough to force any child to grow up in a hurry.

IT WAS long after midnight when the newcomers settled in for the night. Joel and Lanie had scrounged up a meal of ham sandwiches and canned corn for them before making the sleeping arrangements. Lanie was ten years younger than Angie, and she and Joel hadn't gotten around to children yet, so there was plenty of space in their four-bedroom home.

Angie thought she'd drop right off after the exhausting day on the road, but she was so thrilled to be home that her brain wouldn't quiet down. She was lying on the bottom bunk with Neal above her. Allyson was on a spare mattress on the floor.

Angie rolled onto her side and watched Allyson tossing in her sleeping bag. "Are you awake?" she whispered.

Allyson turned to face her, and said, "Yeah. I'm too wound up to sleep. I can't believe you're here, Mom. I knew you'd show up someday, but I didn't think it would be so soon."

"It almost wasn't, and I can't wait to tell you about what I've been through, but I want to know about Nana and Grandpa. Are you able to talk about it?"

"Yes, I am. Grandpa went out to get a pizza the day the CME hit. We figured it might be our last one for a while. We had no idea just how long. The CME wasn't supposed to hit so soon, so Grandpa wasn't worried about going out. He never came back, Mom. We still don't know what happened to him. Nana was crazy with worry. She wanted to go out searching for him, but we didn't want her to leave us alone. Things were pretty wild out there at first. After three or four days, we knew something bad happened to him."

Angie reached over and stroked her hair. "How terrible. I hate that you all had to go through that."

"It sucked so bad. We were so scared for you and Dad, and Grandpa was missing. Not even Nana knew what to do."

"How did you get by in the house with no power?"

"We burned the firewood Dad left for us. We were lucky we didn't have a gas fireplace. People who did had no way to heat their houses. We cooked over the fire, which was what Nana called a novelty at first, but it got old quick. We had no choice but to do it, but it took a lot of work. We moved our mattresses into the family room to sleep so we could stay warm. We always had to keep the fire going. It got so cold here after the CME."

Angie thought back to those horrible first days and could relate. She'd wished ten times a day she could build a fire inside the plane.

"Tell me about Nana," she finally said.

Angie could hear Allyson taking a few deep breaths before continuing. "She got sick about a week after the CME. It was just like a cold at first. Then she got a bad cough. I think it was worse because she was so sad about Grandpa. The cars wouldn't turn on, so I had to walk to try and find help. The hospital was a madhouse, and no one would come, and I didn't know where Dr. Finley lives. A few of the neighbors that were left did what they could, but nothing made her better. Mrs. Norman finally found a doctor who would come check on Nana, but he told us it was too late. He left some antibiotics and a few oxygen tanks that he could spare, but she died when they ran out."

Angie was heartbroken at hearing her poor daughter's story and learning how her mother had suffered before she died. The world had become such a miserable place in so many ways. She remembered what Riley had said about living in the nineteenth century. Her mother was a prime and painful example of what that meant.

"Were you and Neal alone with Nana when she died?"

"No, thank goodness. The Normans brought all three of us to their house. Mr. Norman took care of Nana's burial. We had a funeral for her and Grandpa. It was so sad but beautiful. Shelly Kendrick from church sang a song, and I read a poem I found in one of your books. That gave us closure. That's what Mrs. Norman told us, anyway."

Angie was so touched by Allyson's words. She wiped her face and blew her nose before saying, "She's right. I hope I get the chance to thank the Norman's someday."

"They're not in their old house anymore. When Auntie and Uncle showed up to bring us here, the Norman's told us they were going to live with their son in Philly. They didn't give us the address. When the internet comes back on, we can google them."

"The internet isn't going to come back, sweetheart. Probably ever."

Allyson rolled onto her stomach and propped up on her elbows. "How do you know that?" Angie told her about Dr. Landry and what they'd learned from him about the CMEs. Allyson looked devastated. "We've been waiting for the power to come back on every day. Now, you're saying it never will?"

"Dr. Landry said it could take years or even decades, and the satellites that provide the internet have probably all been destroyed. I'm sorry to have to tell you this, but we'll be living like people lived 150 years ago."

"No more cell phones or texting? No more computers ever? How will we live like that?"

"By doing what we've been doing these past several weeks. How have you been surviving here?"

"Don't you remember that Uncle Joel installed solar panels around Halloween? They kept working somehow when the CME hit. We've had electricity here the whole time. We ride the horses into town to find food and other supplies, and we're going to grow a garden in the spring. Uncle Joel has well water, too."

"There you go, honey. Everything we need to sustain ourselves."

Allyson's lip trembled before she covered her face and broke into tears. "First finding out for sure Dad's gone, and now that the whole world is dark," she said between sobs. "I don't want to live like the olden days. It's such hard work, and I can't contact my friends. I don't even know where they are or if some of them are alive. And what if we get hurt or sick like Nana? We just have to die?"

Angie moved to the floor beside her and put an arm around her shoulder. "Listen to me. It will be that way at first, but humans are resourceful and resilient. It will be hard, but we'll manage." We'll figure things out in time. You'll have some unexpected challenges, but you'll be part of the generation that will get the world up and running again. It'll be a fascinating time of innovation. You're so bright, and I look forward to seeing what you'll accomplish.

Allyson lowered her hands and gazed up at Angie. "Are you just saying that to cheer me up?"

Angie shook her head. "I meant every word with all my heart. We've suffered painful losses and the world we knew is gone. We'll need time to grieve and recover from that. It won't be easy, but there's also still a world of promise ahead. I can't wait to see what we'll make of it."

END

Thanks for reading! If you enjoyed this book, please leave a review at your favorite retailer. Much appreciated!

Find your copy of **SOLAR FURY**, the gold medal winning first book in the ***Shattered Sunlight Series,*** online at your favorite retailer.

About the Author

E.A. Chance is an award-winning writer of suspense, historical, and post-apocalyptic women's fiction who thrives on crafting tales of everyday superheroes.

She has traveled the world and lived in five countries. She currently resides in the Williamsburg, Virginia area with her husband and is the proud mother of four grown sons and Nana to one amazing grand-darling.

She loves hearing from readers. Connect with her at:

https://eachancebooks.com
e.a.chance@eachancebooks.com